# 2012: The Awesome King of Destiny

© 2011 by Byron deVere, St. Clair Publications

ISBN 978-0-9826302-2-8

Printed in the United States of America by
St. Clair Publications
P. O. Box 726
McMinnville, TN 37111-0726

http://stan.stclair.net

# 2012: The Awesome King of Destiny

## Byron deVere

**StCP**

*2012: The Awesome King of Destiny* is purely a work of fiction. Any likeness to any person living or dead is entirely coincidental. This book is not an indictment against the Freemasons, any modern Order of Knights Templar or other organization, church or family.

# Reviews

*2012: The Awesome King of Destiny* is a riveting book that keeps you turning page after page after page.

Amongst the priceless treasures discovered by the Knights Templar was an ancient Gnostic manuscript, a manuscript written during the Midrash by a specially chosen priest of a sect, a number of which settled in Qumran and became the Essenes.

It is this manuscript that prophesizes the messiah-to-come of the New World  Order, courtesy of the following words: *This leader shall be called by a form of Jove, for he shall be great in all the earth. He shall spring from the Royal House of Stewards of the truth. They shall bear the Holy Light, the hidden knowledge of the ages. Their line shall descend from the most royal of families, and there shall be no doubt that he will be a man among men.*

Julian Stuart is that man.  He is also a man who is being manipulated and controlled by an orchestrated agenda.

In a race against time, the reader is propelled into a world that seems impossible to rescue from the docket of chaos that has been put into motion.
-**Michele Doucette**, author of *A Travel in Time to Grand Pré*, *The Ultimate Enlightenment for 2012: All We Need Is Ourselves* and *Veracity at Its Best*

DeVere's *2012: The Awesome King of Destiny* is a whirlwind banquet of intrigue and suspense leaving the reader greedily turning pages for the next morsel. Often feeling predictable only to abruptly snatch the reader back into an entirely unforeseen scenario, deVere has created a sub-genre all his own. Employing his knowledge of current world events, attitudes and diversity – mingled with historic fact, accepted conspiracy and science – deVere has us surely believing we are living the events surrounding Julian Stuart and the World community.

My suggestion: One should approach this tale with the knowledge that no one is safe – nothing is sacred. Be prepared to be completely immersed in the lives of a plethora of believable, 'every man' characters and allow yourself to feel their joy and angst. Most importantly, if you are one who reads the last chapter before completing the book – I would recommend that you tear the last two chapters out and hide them from yourself until you have finished the others.

-**Kent Hesselbein,** author of *Good to the Finish!* and upcoming title: *Crusaders and Heretics – Templars, Freemasons and the Church.*

# Author's Note

Research for this book was begun in 2006, with the actual writing beginning late in 2008. This research also included trips to several locations mentioned in the book.

As you absorb this graphic tale, please be objective, following through to the end before making any judgments. In addition, please remember, it is fiction. Upon arriving at the conclusion, I urge you to ask yourself the riveting question, "Could something like this EVER happen?"

# Chapter One

The placid silence of the night was abruptly invaded by a ghastly, bloodcurdling scream — one that pulsated through the plush Alexandria apartment at a glass-shattering decibel.

Julian Stuart bolted from his king bed, shaking his head in violent motion. Suddenly, the grueling reality hit him: this surreal sound had emitted from the pit of his own stomach! This time, the dream had been so vivid that he could swear it had been a stark reality.

Instantaneously, a petite pinnacle of light broadened beneath his bedroom door, which he had recently decided to secure upon retiring each night. His keen hearing assured him that as sure as hell is hot footsteps were creeping his way just beyond the latched portal. The LCD timepiece on the stand by his resting place read "2:07." In a flash, he donned the mauve silk robe at his feet, and quietly unlocked and shoved up the window. He was out. For once he was glad of the nightmare!

There had been a motive behind his choice of the first floor flat. He had also been keeping his car stocked with a packed suitcase and some basic necessities.

In a dash, the lock had been jimmied, the door was opened, and three shots from a muffled nine mm handgun penetrated the mattress, lodging in the wall. The masked assailant flipped the switch, and stared blankly into an empty bed. The light curtains flitted in the soft April breeze, and the shrill of squealing tires quickly provided his answer.

"Son of a...!" The assassin's utterance froze abruptly as a siren sounded, and blue lights flickered through the open casement.

*How long can I keep up this freaking pace?* Julian wondered. Now he must move again. *Another name change... perhaps a bit of plastic surgery. Maybe John Sinclair was too obvious an alias. J. S.?*

This hadn't been the first attempt on his life, just a different M.O. The initial episode, as he allowed himself to quickly reflect backward, had been the reason for his frantic flight. He was supposed to leave work at 4:30 sharp, as he had for weeks on end without fail. On this particular afternoon, however, he had been detained by a persistent client. When the deafening explosion rocked the office building, he had no clue that it had been his car that had just been blown to smithereens. *Obviously a ti-*

*mer...or it could have been set off by a cell phone or remote from another sector of the city.*

His fun-filled days with his gorgeous bride must have been a part of another allusive lifetime, or they had only existed as a wishful figment of an incredibly lucid imagination. Now alone, running had become a way of life.

As Julian's shiny new silver Jaguar XJ floated westward through the hazy hours of the early morning, he neared the junction of Interstate 66 with 81 south. But his mind was neither on the road, nor his destination.

A maze of ruffled memories flooded his consciousness, and possessed his very soul.

He had been born of an affluent family in Charlottesville. His blueblood ancestors had made Virginia their home since it had been but a colony to the mother country. They had ranged from prosperous planters to ambitious politicians. One of his tenth great-grandfathers had been the first governor, and several had served as state legislators. It had come as no surprise when he had learned that his family had been slave owners, and that his third great-grandfather Stuart had proudly worn the uniform of a Confederate Lieutenant.

11

Being from an unremitting line of Roman Catholic stock, and given his baptism as a wee lad, he had been obliged to attend mass each first day of the week.

As he grew to maturity, however, his thoughts had often trailed to his fancy of the day, with morality taking a backseat. That is, until he had met Klarissa, nearly six years ago, while still in college.

But his retrospection now was confined to his more bizarre discoveries; those which would lead to the contract on his life and his unbidden kismet as a fugitive.

How he sorely wished that he could turn back the clock. He would even give up the national treasury, if he had it, for simple peace of mind; for the elusive dream of living a "normal" life.

From the earliest years he had been acutely aware of his father's membership in the local Masonic Lodge, in which he had held every office except Chaplin. Jordan Stuart had been a part of a great deal of good done in the community, all of which had been further accomplished through the synergic kindness of the lodge brothers to the families of departed members. When he had turned eighteen, Jordan had almost insisted that he become a

Freemason, something he just hadn't been ready for. During Julian's junior year at Yale, however, he had been selected for membership in The Skull and Crossbones Society, a fraternity for elite students—one in which past US Presidents had been a part.

When he was initiated, he was told that he would "die to the world and be born again into the Order." There were only fourteen "blood brothers" besides him in his class. He was warned never to reveal any activity or secret of the fraternity as long as he should live. He never had, and he knew that he never could. At first, he felt like he had become a member of the Mafia. The prestige had made him feel strangely powerful. Though secretly, some activities had made him squirm, he had eventually grown accustomed to them. His dad had shown extreme pleasure when Julian informed him of his selection for the Order.

But the sequence of events which would take place, scarcely within the past six months, had proven to be much more macabre than anything he had experienced in the Order. Heck, he had been a Boy Scout in comparison.

After graduating Summa Cum Laude with a major in law, Julian had quickly passed the bar and become a junior partner in a prominent Richmond firm. His father's connections were powerful, but he had earned it, Julian reasoned.

As he neared the intersection he realized that he was just driving away...a choice must be made... though he knew he would be heading south... *Atlanta or New Orleans?*

The reverberations rang through his brain... "It's almost time."..."The prince must be tuned in very soon." He was remembering only bits and pieces. Evidently, however, they thought he knew something greater.

Atlanta it was. His trusted friend, Sean Mac Lean, would never let him down.

At that hour, in their chic suburban Richmond home, Klarissa Stuart was stirring restlessly. It was as though her subconscious mind was connecting with Julian and telling her that something was amiss.

As she blinked her dainty green eyes, her thoughts went instinctively to the first time she and Julian had met. Julian had not told her for the longest time just how different she was, but Klarissa had been a breath of fresh air. She was so disparate from the party-hungry, sex-crazed playmates which had popped up in every corner of his collegiate life. They had bumped into each other at a social for his father's corporation, Stuart Marketing--quite literally, in fact.

"Oh, sorry!" Julian said, half frowning. His martini had tapped her shoulder, and chilling liquid trickled down her well-bronzed arm.

"No problem," said the voice which melted the steel of his heart.

"Here's a towel," he said. "I haven't seen you around before."

"My dad is a new client of this company."

And so, the two had introduced themselves. From there, it wasn't long till they were dating.

Her father, Dr. Ernest Cline, was an optometrist who had recently relocated in Richmond. He was to become close with Jordan Stuart, both as a client and as a friend.

Julian sped southward on I 81. His mind was a million miles from politics, but presidential candidate billboards flew by on either side. The race was heating up more each week. From his rear, he noticed a pair of brilliant headlights racing in his direction like a bat out of hell. His jaw stiffened as he pushed the pedal to the mat.

At first light Klarissa was ringing her husband's phones; first, the number at the flat, then his iPhone. He had purposely left the cell off. Julian had told no one else, least of all his father, of his whereabouts, or his numbers. He could take no chances. He felt that there was something else which his father had failed to reveal to him when the showdown had come between them. They were in some ways so much alike they were always butting heads. But why would his father hold out on him? What could possibly keep him from unmitigated honesty? While he knew the sinister plot of the powers that be, the identity of the prince was not nearly clear. Perhaps that was it: they thought he could get to the prince.

The first piece of the murky puzzle had fallen into place quite by accident. While conducting online research for a client involving a property dispute, an estate passed down through many generations, Julian had made a remarkable discovery. His client was being sued by a distant cousin who claimed that the estate in question had been wrongfully taken by the brother of the proper heir. According to family tradition, he had hidden the true will of their father, and forged another.

The plaintiff claimed to now have the true will, said to be drafted in the late eighteenth century.

This case had not been reopened since the time of the will. Not only was Julian curious as to why the heirs would be in question after over two hundred years, but the further he delved into the records, the more involved the mystery became.

That was when he found a connection to his own ancestry. George Stuart, his sixth great-grandfather, had been the attorney for the forebear of his client, Saul Stewart Morris.

At first he had given this no second thought. It was only in looking over the land records that he discovered that the Stuart/Stewart family had deeded the property to Morris' parents. George Stuart's purpose as the attorney for the rightful heir was to pass the estate on to the selected protector of the property, as designated by a group, who Julian discovered were all local members of the Masonic Lodge.

Before the reading of the will, however, George had been killed. The identity of the killer had never been proven. And Julian still wasn't sure if his client was even related to his family.

It didn't take a rocket scientist to discern that the certain common denominator was the Freemasons. *Why had he been chosen as the attorney in this case?* That also seemed obvious.

There had to be a reason that this had been a closed case for all of these years. His father owed him an explanation; as a matter of fact, his father owed him a freaking lot of explanations.

He wasn't supposed to figure this out quite so early.

Klarissa vigorously paced the floor. Why in the name of God wasn't Julian answering. She had even sent him a text, and received no response. *I need to call Jordan.* The thought streaked through her mind, and just as rapidly was abandoned because she had been given strict instructions to tell no one about his Alexandria flat. *But, why did he tell me that?* Yet she knew that there was a darn good reason.

# Chapter Two

Jordan sat pensively at his desk, sipping a steaming cup of cappuccino, and checking his email. Quickly he ripped his BlackBerry robotically from its case on his belt.

"Jordan Stuart!"

"Good morning, Your Worship."

"Morning, Montgomery. Skip the humor. You know better than to call me that on the phone. We have a royal problem."

"I told you we should have clued him in on his destiny sooner."

"He's been programmed, just like we were all told must happen. When the time comes, he'll be as docile as a kitten. Remember, had the time been earlier, I would have been in his shoes. Neither of us has any control over destiny."

"How well I know."

"I'm glad you phoned. I'm calling a special meeting of the Grand Priory this evening at 7:30. Call the others. I've got something to attend to."

In Vatican City, a week earlier, the Holy See had been notified that the end-time prophecies of Jesus and John the Revelator were about to come to a climax.

The massive, lavishly appointed, art-splattered *L'uffico de Papa* with its marbled floor, lofty ceiling and ornate chandelier never ceased to amaze Cardinal Jabaldi, though he'd been there scores of times. Not just under the administration of this pope, but those of his two predecessors as well. Pope Pious XIII gazed out the gigantic window as if admiring the spectacular view of St. Peter's Square for the first time.

"Tell me about the prophecies," he finally said, his voice low and almost irritated, but with a strain of feigned interest. "Just how are you so sure that this young man is the one we've been waiting for?"

"In the gospels we have a record of the time, not long before he was arrested, when Jesus' disciples came at him with some pointed questions. They asked him exactly how they would know the signs of the end of the age. His answers were very specific."

"Yes, yes, we all know about the twenty-fourth chapter of the Gospel attributed to St. Matthew, and the parallel in St. Luke's Gospel.

These have been studied by the Church since that day. We all agree that a lot of his prophecies have come to pass. And some prophecies are symbolical. But what points to right now, and more specifically, to the man of whom you speak?"

"First, we must go back to when Jesus was born."

"What on earth are you talking about?"

"His birth is a major key in understanding these prophecies."

"Now you really have me confused."

"We know that he was not born on the traditional date. Constantine hatched up a bunch of holidays, calling them Christian, only to have them align with the pagan holidays already being celebrated within the Roman Empire. One of these was what we the one that we observe as 'Christmas.'"

"Tell me something I don't know."

"Jesus birth is recorded as occurring during the reign of Herod the Great. That places it between eight and four BC. Mary's conception of Jesus was likely around the time when the scriptures record her visit by a heavenly being called 'Gabriel.' In the first chapter of the Gospel of St. Luke, it is recorded that this was in the sixth month. Given the revelation of this knowledge to Zachariah, the father of John the Baptist, and his position in Judaism, it is likely that this referred to Adar, the sixth month of the Hebrew religious calendar. We must also remember that the magi from Persia followed a phenomenal heavenly spectacle to find the Christ Child. This would have meant that his birth had occurred within the Jewish month of Tishra.

"In 1603, Johannes Kepler, a brilliant Dutch astronomer and mathematician, observed a conjunction between Jupiter and Saturn in the Constellation Pisces, noting that by their converging they appeared as a larger, and new, 'star.' Later Kepler recalled the writings of Isaac Abravanel, a Portuguese rabbi who lived from 1436 to 1508. Abravanel stated that Jewish astronomers believed that the messiah would come when there was a conjunction of Jupiter and Saturn in Pisces. In 1925, this hypothesis was reexamined when references to this conjunction were discovered in the cuneiform inscriptions of the archives of the ancient Babylonian School of Astrology at Sippar. This particular conjunction was recorded three times in 7 BC, one of these being Saturday, Tishra 10th, the equivalent of October 3rd. in our Gregorian calendar. Most amazingly, Tishra 10th, in 7 BC, was the Jewish Day of Atonement!"

The Holy See threw his head back and rolled his dark eyes. He could no longer act the least acquiescent. "Fascinating, I'm sure. Are you making a point? I don't have all day!"

"Most definitely, Your Holiness. Please bear with me. It's quite important that you hear me out.

"Contrary to our common teaching that the Church Age started at Jesus' birth, it started at the birth of the Church, the Day of Pentecost."

"Well, well, now. You've finally said something that makes sense. But what in Hades do the birth date of Jesus and the beginning of the Church have to do with the price of eggs in China?"

"These are only keys to date the end of this age; the Church Age. To determine when the age began, we must determine the date of Christ's birth. According to those who wrote about it, he began his ministry at age thirty, and it lasted three years. Dating from 7 BC, and remembering that there was no year zero, then going forward thirty-three years, it stands to reason that the actual crucifixion occurred in

3787 on the Jewish calendar, or 27 AD. Now the fun starts."

"I hope so. I have other plans for this century."

The Pontiff was getting so bored that his mind was drifting to the time when he was six years of age. He was in his first year of parochial school and the Sister was drilling him.

"Why do we celebrate Christmas, Marcus?"

"Because we like getting presents?"

Snickers arose throughout the room. The irritated nun tapped the desk briskly with her rod.

"Marcus, don't try to be humorous! It's called Christmas because we hold a mass in honor of the birth of the Christ Child. He is the reason for the season, don't you ever forget it."

And he hadn't. He had been a staunch advocate of the letter as well as the spirit of the teachings of the Church. It had paid off. He was now God's spokesperson to millions.

The pope shook his head. The cardinal was still talking. He would at least pretend to listen a bit longer.

"It might interest you to know that this is also backed up by the predictions of the Prophet Daniel. The fact that the birth of Jesus was prophesied is undeniable. And the dates of Passover that year fit the scenario. I'll leave it at that."

"Now what are you going to say, the Church sets dates for the end? We would be the laughing stock of the world! This has been done several times, and you know what happened to the others."

"Now that we have established these probable times, let's look at what Jesus told his disciples. I'll give you the Reader's Digest Abridged Version."

"Thank God." The pope sighed deeply. Sitting down, he leaned his head backward and blinked nervously.

"Jesus predicted twelve events which were to take place before the end of the age. Sound familiar? Twelve tribes of Israel, twelve disciples, twelve gates of Jerusalem, and so on. It started with what he called 'false messiahs.' There were a number of these messiahs who didn't deliver down through history. Wars and rumors of wars. Like we can't see that everywhere. Extreme natural disasters; we've had more of those lately than ever in recorded history. False prophets, persecution of Christian believers, preaching all over the world, and what Daniel and Jesus called "the Abomination of Desolation." This eighth sign is to be the be-ginning of the end. It signals the final reign of death around the world. This will be brought on by an awesome king who takes his orders from a mystical spiritual leader, who will at-tempt to destroy the Church."

"So where do your dates come into play."

"In more than one place, Your Holiness. First, there are the prophecies of Daniel, the Apostle Paul and John the Revelator. They point directly to our day. Jesus said that Israel would become a nation again, and that this generation would not die out before the end would come. That happened in 1948, as you know. There are still a considerable number of folk around who were alive in 1948, yourself included.

"There has been a consensus among those believing in these and other prophecies that it would likely come to a head within two thousand years from its beginning. Many have tried to set dates, as Your Holiness has so aptly stated. Not only are Christians and Jews ready for a new era of peace, but all major religions have predicted it. Why were so many wrong about the end events culminating by the year 2,000? Simply because the Church Age didn't start in the mythical year zero. It started in 27 AD. This would likely indicate that end events will take place before 2027.

"St. Paul, in the Second Epistle to the Thessalonians, predicted a leader that would come and proclaim himself as a god. This is equated with the Abomination of Desolation, when the Temple will be turned over to the new world spiritual head, called by some, 'the Anti-Christ.' "

"I have even heard that some people think that I am this so-called 'Anti-Christ.' For sure, early reformers placed this title upon the holy office which I hold."

"Yes, Your Holiness, but we know the fallacy of that teaching, and this is far too real for us to ignore. The Mayan prophecies call for our present age to terminate this year, in 2012. Even a large percentage of psychics feel that the end of this age is very near. A number of groups have, for some time, complied with this time frame. To say that we are near is a gross understatement, but there is a more positive reason to believe that this particular unsuspecting prince is the coming world leader. The one to be controlled by the 'Anti-Christ' system."

"It has never been believed that this man would be an American. I can't see how he could be."

"As the late Paul Harvey told his American audiences, 'and now, the *rest* of the story.' Young Julian Stuart is the direct male heir of a long line of nobles from what was called in Arthurian Legend and Celtic Mythology 'the Fisher King.' Most people were unaware that this group even existed until the late twentieth century. His family was among the original settlers of the Virginia Colony. His ancestors were also heirs to the secrets of the original Knights Templar, not one of those neo-Templar groups which have sprung up in recent years. These kings were descendants of the royal lines of Europe who claimed divine right to rule. They are *proclaimed* by numerous modern authors to be descended from Jesus and Mary Magdalene, as well as the illusive Norse god, Odin. It only makes perfect sense that this line will one day demand their divine right. This is the most pure royal lineage in the world.

"The Church is very fortunate to have an informant, someone closely allied to the prince, who has apprised us of the progress. There is no doubt that he is the one."

"I understand what you are saying." The pope's mouth was dry, and his palms moist with perspiration. "I wash my hands of this matter. As far as I'm concerned, this conversation has never taken place."

# Chapter Three

---

"**S**ean! Thank heavens, you're home!"

"Hey, man! How the hell are you?"

"Don't ask. I was rudely awakened this morning. I need a place to hang till I can get myself together and figure out what's happening to me."

"Sure, man. Come on down. Where are you?"

"I'm on 75, coming up on 285. I'm almost there."

"Hey, hey! I'll tell Lolita I need a break. She's about gotten me over 'lonely' anyway. The last week has been a blast."

"See ya shortly."

"And that's all I know. 'The prince must be tuned in,' what do you make of it?"

"Sounds freakin' uncanny, my friend. Maybe you should catch some z's while I do a little shopping. You just happened to arrive at a good time. I had taken off work to be with Lolita this week. She was a little pissed, but said she understood the 'friend' bit. She just wanted to make sure I didn't have another lover."

"He's in Atlanta. We have to act fast. We can't take any chances."

Jordan closed his eyes, and his Black-Berry. A slight smirk appeared where mere moments before there had been disgust. If he had known what type car Julian was now driving, he would have been able to obtain the pertinent information to track his GPS, not needing to have been put through this hassle.

Thank heavens for small favors. His man had come through.

Sean pulled back into his drive. Julian didn't have a clue, but he wouldn't be leaving on his own.

It was late March, and the glorious dogwood blossoms were beginning to cover Atlanta like a heavy blanket of late snow. Julian awoke, and yawned. He could hardly remember that it was Monday morning. He wondered how Klarissa must feel about the fact that he hadn't called. But he felt safe enough now. He'd let her know that he was in the best of hands. He wanted her to feel that though he was somewhat daunted he could still remain rational.

"Thank God! I've been out of my head with worry. When will I see you?"

"You know it's not safe there. We'll have to figure out something. I miss you too. I've got to know who's trying to kill me, and who this prince is that they're after."

Julian laid down his iPhone and rubbed his eyes. More bits started to come to him, this time from an earlier time frame. He could vaguely remember lying in a large room, much like a hospital, or perhaps a laboratory. Some-one was leaning over him....two people, in fact. One was an older, white-haired man wearing a medical mask, of a sort. They were talking, but the words seemed as if they were in a wind tunnel. Then the younger one, a blond man in a dark suit and tie, was speaking directly to him. Yes, it was coming back! "Hang in there, my prince. You will change the world."

*"My prince?"* What on earth was he re-calling? Surely *he* could not be the prince. Was Jordan not his real father?

"Good morning, Julian! You slept about twelve hours. Have some coffee. How do you like it?"

"Oh, just a little cream and arsenic."

Sean smiled and poured the coffee. Julian didn't know how close he was.

"I don't have to tell you what happens if your man fails again." Cardinal Jabaldi scowled as he bellowed into the phone. "The prophecies are irrefutable and explicit. The time is resolute for the Awesome King to arrive on the scene. It was determined thousands of years ago. Unless…"

"Unless *what*?"

Well, we know that all prophecies are subject to change. Even God can change his mind."

"Just what makes you so freaking sure?"

"We have scripture for it."

"And just who canonized the 'scripture?'"

"Shut up and do your job! This king will end the Church as we know it.

"Only Jesus Christ, himself can save us then."

"Exactly. And this can't happen on my watch."

Jabaldi had two contacts. This one who wanted the king dead, the other who only wanted the coronation stopped. The latter was a fiery, outspoken female who refused to divulge her name.

Klarissa sighed and put the cordless phone back on the hook. One piece at a time, her dainty lingerie dropped to the bathroom floor, and she stepped gingerly into the opiate Jacuzzi, first cautiously testing the temperature with the big toe of her right foot. The bubbles felt so sublime that she almost fell asleep.

In a majestic London Penthouse, General Seton Loraine quickly punched the number.

"Jordan Stuart, good morning."

"Well? Can I pop open the champagne yet?"

"We've got everything under control. The prince is safe, and will be en route to Jerusalem soon."

"Great. The council will assemble there at ten hundred hours tomorrow morning, local time. Don't forget the manuscript."

"You have my word on it. I'm packed and ready. Not even the missus will suspect a thing."

"See you there. You know where to meet."

Cardinal Jabaldi bit his lower lip. Did he dare tell the Pontiff the whole truth? Did he dare tell him that a secret ancient Gnostic manuscript was the most explicit source of the prophecies of the Awesome King? Should he tell the pope that it even foretold his name and the precise time of his arrival? Should he tell him that he had seen actual digital photos of it, and that the translations were unquestionably accurate?

*No,* he thought. *Some things are unspeakable.* He would just continue his earnest quest for the manuscript. He would nullify its authenticity, or better yet, burn it. *Nessun manoscritto, nessuna profezia,* he thought. With no manuscript, the prince would be just as unconvinced of his destiny as the pope had been of the biblical prophecies.

# Chapter Four

---

**A**s Julian opened his eyes, he could barely detect the soft whirring of jet engines. It was the Lear. This was a very special Lear with extra fuel capacity designed for cross-oceanic flights. He'd been aboard this plane numerous times.

"Dad?!"

"Yes, my son."

"What's going on? Where are you taking me? I've been drugged."

Suddenly Julian was alert. "Damn! Sean did this! I can't trust anybody. All I can ask is why?"

"My son," Jordan said calmly. "I first want to say how sorry I am that I have not been able to reveal all of this to you before. You are a most special individual. Your birth was no accident. Your destiny was prophesied thousands of years ago…"

"Stop right there! I don't believe in any freaking prophesies. You're scaring the hell out of me."

"Son, I know exactly how you feel. I would feel the same way if I were you."

"I've been having some eerie flashbacks. They seem more like I've been hallucinating; something about a *prince*."

Jordan smiled. "Your birth was arranged long ago. I can only now relate this to you, because the time is right. When you were at Yale, you were a member of a secretive fraternity called the Skull and Crossbones Society."

"So?"

"Your invitation to that Order was not coincidental. And you know, of course, that I am a Freemason. What you're not aware of is the fact that not only am I a thirty-third degree Mason, and a member of the Supreme Council, but I am the Grand Prior in the United States for a very exclusive order known as the True Knights Templar. The Masons were merely a stepping stone. We are the keepers of the secrets given to the original Templars. Not only that, but you are a direct descendant of the Holy Blood Royalty, the bloodline of Jesus and Mary Magdalene."

Julian took a deep breath. He did all but literally bite his tongue. He knew now that his father had most assuredly gone off the deep end. But he also realized that he must be ex-tremely cagy in his reply. He felt that anything he said could and would be used against him in the court of life.

"Go on."

Jordan sighed. "I'm so happy that you are listening to me. I can't tell you how much anxiety I've had over what this revelation would bring."

"Are you even really my father?"

"Oh yes, my son, most assuredly so."

"What does Mom think of all of this?"

"She doesn't know."

"What do you mean, 'she doesn't know?'"

Jordan eased his head back, blinked, and sighed again. "This isn't easy either."

There was a pregnant pause which seemed to Julian to last an eternity. "Your 'mom' isn't your biological mother…"

Julian wished he were dead. Anger welled up inside as if his stomach were a boil-ing cauldron. "I can't talk about this anymore! You've lied to me all my freaking life! And I can't believe that Mom lied to me too! Just take me home. Klarissa and I will find a way to live our lives free of your hypocrisy."

"Mom didn't lie to you. She thinks that you're her natural son. We'll talk about that later. You have to face it, my son. It's your destiny. And you're forgetting something in your haste. Our enemies are after you. They want nothing less than to assassinate you. What good will that do your beloved Klarissa?"

Julian lunged for his father. His fists pounded violently against his chest. "My life is over! You have taken away all I care about!"

"No, my son, your life has not yet begun, you are about to be born again into your rightful position as ruler of the world."

Julian was too confused and upset to ask more questions. But they were as an army, invading his mind, and overflowing its borders.

How could the woman he had called his mother not know? Who was his birth mother? Who the hell was trying to kill him? Where were they going? And more importantly, how could he escape?

# Chapter Five

It was April 2nd, the Monday before Easter, and Atarot Airport was overflowing. All of Jerusalem was abuzz with Christians who had made the Holy Week pilgrimage. The Lear was cleared to land at the private strip designated for dignitaries and VIPs.

Jordan gazed into the eyes of his especial son.

"Everything is more than OK. I know that you don't see it now, but the world is yours, just receive it."

"I need to be with Klarissa." Julian chose his words carefully.

"We know. It's being arranged."

Klarissa reached sleepily for the alarm, but it was the phone instead.

"Mrs. Stuart?"

"Yes."

"This is Chief Mike Montgomery with the Police Department in Richmond. I apologize for calling so late, but I have news regarding your husband."

"News? What do you mean? Is he OK?"

"Oh, yes 'am, he's fine. I was just asked to call you and let you know that he is expecting you to join him. He said it is important."

By now Klarissa was wide awake. Something didn't feel Kosher. And that voice....Julian had explicitly told her that neither of them would contact the police.

"Join him where?"

"Oh, he said that we should not speak of his location on the phone. I'm having the local police department send out a plain white wrapper...uh, unmarked SUV to collect you. He told us to be very discreet since there is someone tailing him."

Klarissa intuitively took a coy stance. "Fine. I can be ready in thirty minutes."

Mike Montgomery hung up. Under his breath he mumbled, "They'll be there in twenty."

Klarissa spun animatedly into action. She had not a moment to loose. Sixteen minutes and forty seconds later she was easing her ebony Beamer onto the freeway and heading for Atlanta.

"Pick up, Julian! Where the hell are you?"

*My God! What's happening?* Klarissa could imagine everything. He would have his phone on 24/7.

She rejected the notion of going to her parents. That would be the next place Montgomery would try.

Moments later her Droid cell rang. She let out a muffled sigh of relief.

"Klarissa, I turned my phone off. Listen, I only have a minute. I'm in the restroom at Jerusalem International Airport..."

"Jerusalem, what the hell are you doing in Israel?"

"Just listen! Sean turned me in to Dad. They're trying to set me up as a...forget it, I don't have time. This is too unreal to explain right now. Call Roger Snowden in New Orleans. I can't think of anyone else you might be able to trust. Tell him to check out the 'True Knights Templar.' They are a secretive worldwide organization with powerful connections. There is to be a meeting here today. See what he can find out. Love you. Later."

Klarissa's head was in a blinding whirl. Roger's number was programmed into her Droid.

"Klarissa? Did you look at your watch? It's midnight here, so it's got to be 1:00 there!"

"Roger, how well I know. I'm headed your way. Julian is in trouble. He's been kidnapped and is in Jerusalem."

"No way!"

"Way. This is for real. He wants you to check out the 'True Knights Templar.' He says they are meeting in Jerusalem today, well, I guess it's already tomorrow there, and they're making plans for him, of some kind."

"Holy Mother of God!" I'm already familiar with them. They are the military wing of the modern Illuminati!"

"I'm afraid you've lost me already. Illuminati? What's that?"

"The Illuminati, sister, control the world's currency. Control the money, control the world. Most academics think they are only a long-dead cult. But I, unfortunately, know the truth. I would give anything to just be blissfully ignorant. They are the force behind the world banks. When the bank failures came in 2008 to 2009, they were the instigators of it. They have infiltrated all of the prominent governments, and every major organization and corporation in the world. The top families through the eons have been secretly in charge. The Rothschilds, the Bilderbergers, and the Habsburg dynasty. You don't want to mess with that bunch! I've got friends in low places who can help us, though. Come on down. It will be great to see you! It's been what? Over two years?"

"A while, that's for sure."

Klarissa had only fond thoughts of Roger and Gloria. He and Julian had been roommates at Yale, and had stayed in touch. Roger had even become close with Julian's parents.

He and Jordan shared a lot of personal interests, and had played golf together on many occasions. At one time he had felt closer to Jordan than Julian. But more recently, when Julian had spoken with him, Roger had said that he had not heard from Jordon.

Roger's brilliance in the field of computer science had plunged him into his own business, setting up computer systems for major clients around the globe. This vocation had granted him a fair number of international connections.

He had been Julian's best man, and Klarissa had taken immediately to his Gloria.

She had even promised to be Gloria's matron of honor when they married. But the time had not yet come, as they had both resisted the rigid commitment of marriage.

Cardinal Jabaldi grimaced and jumped. Dressed only in the garb of a common cleric, he had decided to take a pensive walk to mull over his options, and had been narrowly missed by a FedEx truck swerving to avoid hitting a stray dog.

It was a brisk spring morning, and a steady, cold drizzle forced the cardinal into the nearest door: a pub. He was not unhappy that it had thus worked out, because he felt that he badly needed a drink. With the advent of the king so near, his nerves were severely frayed.

As he ordered a whisky sour, he asked himself how a man who had been so near to being elected Pope in the last conclave had become an alcoholic. In spite of all of his efforts, he was no nearer to a conclusion on how to locate Julian Stuart. It was as if he had vanished from the face of the earth.

# Chapter Six

---

Jordan slowly turned and whispered into a hidden mike, "It' time. Tune him in."

"Done."

Julian's countenance suddenly radiated as if the daystar had risen within him.

"Hi, Dad! I'm so excited about what we've been discussing on the trip over. Klarissa is going to be so pleased when I explain to her that we are to be the first family of the One World Union. She will make a lovely queen."

"Yes, my son. The world will finally be at peace."

"It seems like everything is clear, at last. I can't imagine how I could have felt so confused. I've been in training for months, now."

"That you have, son."

"It all seemed like a dream."

"It was very real; your time had just not come. The powers that be are behind you, and now, your higher self will guide you. At the meeting this morning, in half an hour, you will meet your team. You have the finest expert in every field aboard. We haven't left the smallest stone unturned. Excuse me, please; I have a personal call coming in."

"Stuart, this is Mike Montgomery. The 'queen bee' has escaped the hive."

"My god, man! What happened?"

"When our plain wrapper got there, the place was vacant. We were even ten minutes early."

"It's a damn shame that I can't do everybody's job for them, but I haven't become a god yet."

"And you aren't likely to."

"That car has a GPS. And you can track her cell, for heaven's sake. Do your freakin' job!

"Yes, Your Worship. She's on I 59 going into Alabama. We'll stay on her tail."

"Don't loose her, and for the love of the goddess, stop calling me that!"

Jordan knew that he would not have had to face the conflict with Julian; they could have tuned him in immediately upon his entry to the Lear. He just felt better finding out his true feelings. But now, the altercation would be no more. Julian's memory banks were operative, and he understood his mission and his origin.

He even knew that his biological mother was the high priestess of the Order of the Holy Grail, Maria de Sancto Claro. She was the pre-destined mother of the ultimate god-king. The female lineage must be undeniably pure. She was of the original Sancto Claros.

"Jabaldi!" He answered his cell with a snap.

"This is you know who. Julian is in Jeru-salem. He's meeting his team today. They will plan his coming-out party."

"Why the hell haven't I heard from you sooner? You've kept me in suspense till I'm crazy! Why was he not stopped?"

"You don't understand yet, do you? It's not that easy to stop him! I can't just go up against the powers that be. We have to be sub-tle about our moves. I know this is trite, but Rome wasn't built in a day, and the Awesome King won't be taken down just because we wish it so.

"But without you I wouldn't even have known about the manuscript, or anything of this god-forsaken plan. I don't know whether to kiss you or shoot you."

"How about neither? It will be more easily carried out in a public place. That way, we will have access without vulnerability.

They won't be able to prevent it. Stun him and have him captured, but *don't* kill him. There has to be a way. Just make sure you keep him from becoming king."

"And another thing, what is your name? Why have we not met?"

"Did I not provide you with unquestionable evidence, Your Eminence? "

"Yes. I have no doubt as to the reality of the threat, but doing business with a ghost doesn't fit my definition of common sense."

"Be patient, Your Eminence. In due time, I will reveal myself. Let's just say that I also have good reason to want to stop this coronation from happening.

"Can you give me a location where his highness is now?"

"Didn't I just tell you that the time sucks? Be patient. The wisest king ever said, 'For everything, there is a season.'"

*Don't kill him, huh? Who does she think she is kidding?*

"General, it gives me great honor to present to you our prince, His Royal Highness, Julian Stuart."

"The honor is indeed mine. You know that I have actually met you before, but, of course you could not be addressed as the prince then. It was when you and your family were in London on holiday in 1987. Your Highness was but a lad."

"General Lorraine! It is you, isn't it?"

"Yes, Your Highness. I have awaited this occasion from my youth. And so have you, though you were not consciously aware of it. There are reasons for all things. The great puzzle of destiny is now solved, and the gestalt of the ages shall be unveiled. Soon, the world shall be no longer the same. John Lennon envisioned this day. I was with him right after he wrote the classic song, *Imagine*. He knew of our day, though he never lived to see it."

# Chapter Seven

---

Klarissa yawned as she stepped from the shower and reached for the towel. Quickly she dried and dressed. The night had been anything but easy. A knock at her motel door was another red flag.

"Just a minute. Who's there?"

"Housekeeping."

"Come back in about twenty minutes, please, I'm not decent."

*A man with a British accent in housekeeping at a Mississippi motel? Who does he think he's fooling? He sounds a bit familiar.* Klarissa almost laughed out loud, but the stakes were too high to let her hand show. She knew that whoever was outside that door wasn't going anywhere. Quietly, she picked up the in-room phone and dialed 0.

"Front desk."

"Hi, this is Klarissa Stuart in room 249. Do you have a British gentleman in housekeeping? There's one at my door right now."

"Certainly not. Sit tight, I'll call 911."

"Ma'am, there was no one out here when we arrived," the officer drawled. "Ya sure ya weren't imaginin' somethin'?"

"No sir! I know what I heard. I don't expect you to believe me, because you don't understand my situation. My husband is the victim of international kidnapping, and now someone's after me, too!"

"Yes 'am. I think you're into somethin' that may be a tad bit out of our jurisdiction around here. We're a peaceful little southern town, and don't need no bad press. So you just go on and get outta here, ya heah?"

"Oh, I hear you loud and clear, officer! I'm on my way. I'm sorry I had to interrupt your morning coffee!"

Klarissa stomped toward her car, mumbling curses under her breath.

A torch-red Corvette Grand Sport came streaking around Klarissa's jet black BMW. She jerked her head, and steadied the wheel. Still on I 59, she had only been out of Hattiesburg about half an hour.

Suddenly a handgun appeared in the front passenger's window of the 'vette, and a shrill shot rang out through the stillness, barely missing the right front tire of the Beamer.

Luckily, an exit lay just ahead. A second shot pierced the fender, lodging in the firewall insulation. Just as the scarlet Corvette passed the exit, Klarissa swerved rapidly, narrowly escaping.

"Damn it to hell!" the shooter yelled.

"We need to send that little bitch there, not us!" the driver railed in disgust. The next exit is five miles, and I'm not too keen on jumping concrete medians.

Julian was escorted into a building with a prodigious sign reading "World Bank." Below was the Hebrew.

# הבנק העולמי

A maze of corridors led to a plain-looking elevator door. A sign was on the door in Hebrew.

*What the hell?* Julian frowned.

"Admittance restricted," Jordan said.

Jordan placed his right thumb on a scanner beside the door silently granting them entrance. The elevator plunged down, down. Ten floors! In what seemed slow motion a magical sterile world gradually appeared. The scene before Julian was one which he could never have fathomed. The bunker was as posh as Nero's Golden Palace. In fact, it had been designed after its pattern. When half of the palace had reopened in 2007 as a tourist attraction, a photographer for the Illuminati architect had snapped over a hundred digital photos in order to adequately duplicate its radiant historical splendor. But this place was as fresh as a daffodil unfolding in spring and as spic-and-span as an operating room in an unused hospital.

After negotiating another maze of passageways to the Grand Meeting Room, Julian glanced upward at the frescoed vaulted ceiling. *Such charm and precision.*

Julian immediately recognized the duplication of the first century palace architecture and marveled. Long before his marriage, he, Klarissa and Jordon had been among the initial visitors to the Palace of Nero in 2007. Seeing this arresting copy brought a rush of feelings back, and a pulsating desire for his mate.

The rest of the dream team was already assembled before their arrival.

"This, Your Highness, is the actual manuscript about which you were told during your training."

Julian recognized the speaker as the older, gray-haired doctor from his foggy memories of the missing time slots.

"It was recovered from beneath the ruins of the Temple initially built by King Solomon," the doctor continued.

"In fact, the original Templars found many priceless treasures there; much of the gold which had once graced the Temple, genealogies, and other ancient manuscripts. But the most shocking and important of all was this one. It is a Gnostic prophecy which was brought here and buried after the Babylonian exile. It was written during the Midrash by a specially chosen priest of a sect, a number of which settled in Qumran and became the Essenes during the Dark Ages."

Julian sat, calm and mesmerized as the doctor continued.

"It was earlier thought that no prophets came during the four-hundred-year period before the birth of Jesus. This was not true. During this time, members of this sect lived in the wilderness around Qumran. But no duplicate of this manuscript was ever found. That's because its location was securely guarded by the keepers of the Holy Bloodline. No copies were allowed to be produced by their scribes.

"This bloodline existed long before the birth of Jesus. It had come down through the rebel royals of Judah, and was kept in an impregnable locale. These individuals were of the Holy Priesthood of Melchizedek, the priesthood which is stated in the Bible that Jesus represented. The Levites were furious that Jesus claimed to be the heir to the royal priesthood, when he was of the Judaic lineage, rather than being a Levite Cohen. These Cohens, or k-o-h-e-n-s are claimed to be descendants of Zadok, thus the true priesthood.

"Allow me to read the English translation of this amazing text: 'Early in the year of 5773, in the month of Nisan, a great leader shall discover his destiny. He shall be called the true messiah, and shall deliver the people from great perils. The consciousness of man will undergo adroit changes like never before. This leader shall be called by a form of Jove, for he shall be great in all the earth. He shall spring from the Royal House of Stewards of the truth. They shall bear the Holy Light, the hidden knowledge of the ages. Their line shall descend from the most royal of families, and there shall be no doubt that he will be a man among men...'

"Julian is a form of Jove. Stuart is the modern form of steward. Your birth mother is of the family of Sancto Claros, meaning the "Holy Light." They are the keepers of the esoteric knowledge of the ages. Your Highness, this is the reason that you are who you are."

"I am who I am."

"You have spoken it. But as yet, this revelation is between those of our group who are meant to understand. For the rest of the world, our message is still to be in riddles. In the Bible they were called parables."

"I understand, Father."

"I know you do."

"And Klarissa?"

"She will join us. The two of you shall soon be united as one."

"Thank you, Father."

# Chapter Eight

---

"**K**larissa!"

"Hello, my love. Your father made it possible for us to be reunited!"

"I can't believe you're really here! Have you been told about our glorious future?"

"Of course, my love! We don't have to worry about anyone getting to us now. We are being protected by the powers that be."

Julian smiled. "We *are* the powers that be."

"By Jove, you're so right!" The look in her eyes was one of expressive pleasure, and her smile was that of the Cheshire cat.

As Klarissa wound down the final leg of her trek into the city, her thoughts wandered to the last time that she and Julian had seen their friends. It was February 7, 2010, and the entire nation had been riveted with unusually heavy snowfalls. The couples met in Miami, where the weather was considerably more pleasant.

Roger was jubilant because the Saints, which had never played in a Super Bowl in the history of their franchise, were finally facing off against the Indianapolis Colts in Super Bowl 44.

The game had proved to be an edge-of-the-seat thriller. Thanks to an unbelievable interception by Tracy Porter in the fourth quarter, the New Orleans spectacular 31 to 17 victory was clinched. Roger had been so keyed up that night that he could hardly sleep.

"I'm glad you escaped those goons!" The look on Roger Snowden's face let Klarissa know that Julian had chosen wisely this time. Thank God she had made it to New Orleans.

"I'm not sure we're safe yet. Those 'goons' are likely law enforcement officers. They have tracking ability. I turned off my cell phone and jerked the wires loose on the GPS. Luckily, I didn't have one built into this car.

"I knew that Julian could leave a message if he had the chance to try and call."

"I'm afraid the news is *not* good. Well, the only good news is that I am one of the best hackers in the world. And I run a mean search spider. I have at least been honorable, and not used it to divert funds illegally."

"So, what have you found out?"

"The Illuminati and their covert military wing, the True Knights Templar, have in their possession a one-of-a-kind manuscript which they claim was found by the original Templars during the Crusades."

"What's that got to do with Julian?"

"Absolutely everything. That Gnostic kabalistic manuscript seems to predict that our Julian is to rule the world!"

Klarissa felt the blood draining from her head as her body crumbled to the floor.

"Klarissa! Klarissa! Wake up! 911, this is Roger Snowden, I obviously don't have to tell you my address. I have a young lady here who has just undergone traumatic shock. Please send an ambulance."

"Is she conscious?"

"I'm afraid not."

Jabaldi heard his cell ringing, but barely realized what was happening. The alcohol was doing its job. "Hello."

"We've got a man on the premises at the Shalom Resort in Jerusalem, next to the World Bank building. The conference was held somewhere in that bank. It has evidently just broken up. He has placed a bug in the limo which will be used to transport Stuart and his father about town."

"Just stay in touch."

"You got it. Catch you later."

The cardinal allowed the tense muscles in his face to relax somewhat. Slowly he stepped off the barstool and disappeared into the dense night.

The impressive squad of black Mercedes S Class Luxury Limos each signaled, and one by one, pulled from the lot. The lynx-eyed assassin watched until he was certain that he would be undetected, and then followed. His only intention at this point was to listen for pertinent information. But inwardly, however, he thirsted to kill. His time would come, he reasoned. He could wait a while for the thrill. It would only intensify his pleasure.

Julian could hardly wait to hold Klarissa in his arms that night and make love to her. The "Klarissa" who was with him was all too eager to be an active participant.

"This is unbelievable," Klarissa said, drinking in the website to which Roger had directed her.

"It says that various groups from all over the world, both religious and physic, are predicting vast changes this year. I knew I had heard something about this. Yes, I saw a special on TV in February after an asteroid had come close to earth! They were talking about the predicted true beginning of the New Age. Of course there was that movie a few years back, '2012.' But I didn't bother to see that. You know, I just don't usually pay things like this much attention. It's like the horoscope. I read it sometimes, just for the heck of it, but I don't live my life by it."

"Yeah, I don't even read it. I guess it's more of a chick thing."

"Not necessarily. I've known several guys who didn't want to get out of bed if their horoscope told them they were going to have a rough day."

"No crap?"

"For real!"

"Read the rest of that. About the Mayan prophecies, I mean."

"It says that the ancient Mayan calendar comes to a halt early in 2012, then starts up again on December 21st. Isn't that the Winter Solstice, or something?"

"You got it! There are festivals all over the world to celebrate this every year. This year is bound to be the granddaddy of all Winter Solstices! Many have predicted December 21$^{st}$ as the end of the world as we know it."

After the paramedics had arrived, Klarissa had gradually revived. They had stayed until it was certain that she was in no real danger. She felt safe around Roger. There was just an aura about him that seemed to act as a magnet, and a shield against danger. Maybe she just had a thing for him that she had never admitted. No, she couldn't think that way. She shook her head and spun around.

"Hi, Klarissa!" Gloria had gotten home from work and hung her keys on the wall next to the door. The two hugged and laughed. Roger had called her and given her a brief explanation of Klarissa's fragile state of mind.

"Are you going to be OK?" Roger asked.

"I'll be better just knowing that the two of you are around."

"We wouldn't miss a chance to spend time with you for the world; we only wish it were not under these circumstances," Gloria said.

"That makes three of us." Klarissa smiled and flopped onto the couch.

# Chapter Nine

---

The conference had centered around the rapid-firing events which would take place that year in preparation for Julian's coronation on the Stone of Scone at Winter Solstice.

That night, the new Klarissa covered Julian with hot kisses. Hungrily, he devoured her advances. It was as if they were together for the very first time, he thought. They panted for greater heights as they were rapt in their mutual desires.

*Where had this passion come from?*

He didn't even pretend to care. All that mattered was that it existed. In one day he had become the heir to the world, and the husband of a sex kitten! His dreams were being fulfilled at their highest level of fantasy.

"How in the hell did you let her get away again?"

"She's no dummy, boss. She took an exit right behind us. We couldn't get off for twenty more miles!"

Mike Montgomery would have loved to jump through the phone. "You bloody idiot! Don't you think I know better than that? And what about the tracking device?"

"She disabled the GPS, and the phone went dead."

"I should have known better than to send a couple of jackasses to do a man's job! You're both so fired! I'll handle this my frikin' self!"

Jabaldi paced the floor. *What do I have to do to get this stopped? There has to be a better way.*

"Ring, phone!" he yelped, as if the inanimate electronic device could voluntarily answer back.

The morning had found him with a lamentable, pounding headache. But the hangover was not the extent of his worries.

His deep preoccupation with the imminent crowning of a king who would destroy everything which kept him going was the capstone of his priority list. The phone finally responded.

"We have eight months. Lorraine is holding the first news conference this Saturday in London."

"Do you think this will be the time we are looking for?"

"Don't get your boxers in a twist. Let me get back to you on this."

"I don't wear boxers, and my briefs are already in the worst kind of a twist! We can't wait too long to make our move. The more world support there is for this puppet, the worse it will be. He is their fair-headed boy, and according to the prophecies, he's the only one who can initiate the changes they're calling for. We have to take him out at the first chance!"

"I'll be in touch."

"This is Sarah Sumner with BBC reporting from London, where today a special press conference is being held."

"General Lorraine, the purpose of this conference has been somewhat of a mystery. Please tell our viewers why the shroud has been hanging over it. Is there some sort of announcement that you are making today?"

"Yes, Sarah. As everyone knows, though conditions improved after the bailouts by the US government and concessions made by other nations in the last few years, the unrest has not gone away. There are some economists who are saying that a gigantic move of world opinion is necessary to bring global peace. The North American Union proposed in 2008, and established in late 2011, between the US, Canada, and Mexico, with much protest from the Tea Party, was but the second step, the first having been the European Union, of course, in the effort which has been organized by those remarkable individuals who have had a heart to bring global peace for decades. We are on the threshold of the most sweeping economic and social reforms that have ever happened in our modern world.

"What would it mean if we didn't have to worry when we traveled across borders that we would not be able to have protection by the government? What would it mean if we didn't have to worry about the devaluation of our various currencies against other world monies? Our world money system is still very shaky. I am here to announce that a brilliant young leader is emerging, one who speaks like no other, and is offering workable solutions to these and other problems. There are already negotiations beginning with all heads of state in not only the free world, but also China, North Korea, Israel, Egypt, and even Iran, Pakistan, and other Arab republics. We realize there is still a threat from terrorists in nations like Afghanistan and Yemen. But their governments are cooperating and have joined with us to form a peace-keeping force which is working to lesson that threat. Because of this, the US has agreed to remove all sanctions in these Arab republics. We are gearing up for the greatest meeting of world leaders since the G20 London Summit in April, 2009 — more effective than Toronto in 2010 and Cannes in November 2011 put together — and one which promises to be unparalleled in world history. A date is not yet set, but it will be soon."

Cheers and whistles radiated from the surrounding throngs.

"And just who is this masterful leader of whom you are so hopeful?"

"I am not at liberty as of yet to reveal that information. Security is tight, as I am sure you understand, but before long, the whole world will know."

"General..."

"No more questions at this time, please."

Rumbles were heard throughout the crowd in Westminster. The throngs pressed in, but the General was quietly whisked away.

"Jabaldi, are you there, Jabaldi!" but there was no answer. In the bustling London mass, the cardinal muttered profanely as he endeavored to escape.

# Chapter Ten

Roger Snowden quickly punched in the number.

"Hello."

"Hey, Jim. It's Roger. How ya doin', my man?"

"Just headed for work, busy day, and you?"

"I know that you have all sorts of connections. I've found out that there are some weird things going on right now with the resurrected Illuminati. Can you meet with me and help me make some sense of this mess? Do you know more than I do?"

His query was met with stunned muteness. "Jim? Are you still there?"

"Roger, I seem to be loosing you. You know how these silly cell phones are. I'll catch you later."

That night, about 7:30, Gloria answered the door bell. "Hey, Jim, Roger will be out in a sec. This is a friend of ours, Klarissa Stuart."

"Hi Klarissa, good to meet you."

"Likewise, I'm sure."

"Hey, Jim. Glad you dropped by. I really need to talk to you."

"Yeah. Can we go somewhere and be alone?"

"You can talk in front of the ladies. In fact, Klarissa is why we need to talk."

"No, you don't understand. We definitely need to talk in private."

Klarissa squirmed nervously, but kept her mouth zipped.

"OK, man, I catch your drift. Come into my study."

Roger's study was his own private world. Its walls were brimming with bookshelves chocked full of technical publications and yellow and black "Dummy" books on various subjects. His 2012, fully up-to-the-last-minute Mac Computer, however, took top priority. His mahogany desk was stacked with scrawled notes which only he could hope to decipher.

"I don't know how you even knew that the Illuminati had resurfaced, but watch who you ask. In fact, it would be a good idea to just forget that you ever heard of them. These people are somebody that you don't want to get anywhere near, Roger. They control the

destiny of the world. Not just the money mar-
kets, but the results of elections, and who is
taken out of the picture. You might say they
are like the global CIA, in that respect."

"Well, I already have a considerable
knowledge about them." Roger was beginning
to wonder if he should admit what he really
did know. "And what about their military
wing, the True Templars?"

"Oh, God, Roger. Didn't you hear a
damn word I said? How do you know about
them?"

"Let's just say I get around, but there is
a lot that is still unclear."

"If you must know, listen and then remember what I told you. Forget about it. The
True Templars are just what their name im-
plies. As you are no doubt aware, in the elev-
enth century, the Poor Knights of Christ were
formed in Europe as a group of celibate war-
rior-monks, whose mission was to protect the
Holy Land from Muslim invaders, and keep
Christians safe on pilgrimages to Palestine.
Over the next two hundred years plus, these
knights became more and more numerous, and
extremely powerful. In fact, they became the
bankers of Europe, and a threat to the Catholic
Church and European monarchs. King Phillip

IV of France, also known as Phillip the Fair, and Pope Clemet V agreed that the Order must be dissolved. On Friday, October thirteenth, 1307, Phillip ordered that all Templars within his territories be arrested and accused of vile crimes against Christendom, including homosexuality and worshiping a mysterious head called 'Baphomet.' However, a good number of them escaped, fleeing to Scotland.

"Some of these joined other orders, but some did not. They formed another secret organization known as the True Templars. More than one group claims connection to these original knights, but there is only one Order which fills the bill. The *privileged* Freemasons are privy to their existence, and keep their secrets only in the top rank of their number. What is most incredible is the fact that they escaped with the treasures and secrets, which have remained with them to this day. One of the secrets was the 'Holy Bloodline.' But another secret, which is only known by the top of our order, is going to be revealed this year. I would not tell you this if I did not feel that you are able to be trusted. We've been friends a long time. This can *absolutely* go no further. Also, I know who you are harboring. After your call this morning, I put two and two together, and I had someone check out the cars in your driveway. Klarissa Stuart is the wife of Julian Stuart. Julian is the key to this Templar secret. I came to warn you as a friend, I'm obligated to inform the powers that be of any information that will further the cause. I will have to let them know where she is if she is still here in the morning. I'm only offering you this break once. End of conversation."

Roger sighed deeply. "I hear you. Thanks." *Our order? Oh, my God!* Roger's blood ran cold. Jim Jarvis was a True Templar! He was glad he hadn't mentioned the manuscript.

In his new state of mind, Julian was all that his father had dreamed he would be. He was confident, willing, and more than able.

Now, with "Klarissa" by his side, he would face his destiny with jubilance.

# Chapter Eleven

---

"I can't explain, Klarissa, but you have to leave."

Klarissa frowned. "It's Jim, isn't it? My God, it's obvious! He said something that made you want to turn me out in the cold! How could you?"

Gloria scowled. "What the hell is wrong, Roger? You're as white as a sheet! You can't treat Klarissa like this!"

"Look, it's not what you think! All I can say is that Klarissa is in grave danger if she stays here. We've got to do something at once. Gloria, what about your mother's condo in the French Quarter? The one she has listed in a business name?"

"I know she wouldn't mind you staying there, Klarissa. It's stocked with plenty of food. That will get you by till we can get other arrangements made."

"I think it might be best if you didn't take your BMW. I'll store it for you, at least till we have a plan. I'll call you a cab. Here's the address on Chartres."

The fog, now rare where once a near certainty, had lifted somewhat, and London was abuzz. It was 10:00, Saturday morning, April 21st. A convention of top insurance producers was touring the Temple Church on the DaVinci Code Tour.

General Lorraine was addressing key members of the planning committees for the One World Union at the Royal Horseguards.

Jabaldi sat smugly by the speaker. *Yes, the bug is working!*

"Ladies and gentlemen, this summit was called today because it combines the first day of Abib with the Baha'i celebration of Ridvan, which began, of course, at sunset last evening. We are deeply indebted to the leaders of the Baha'i faith for their undying efforts to unite all major religions.

"United we stand, divided we fall. But we have no reason to fall. Our efforts are nearing fruition. When our dreams are realized, those so aptly expressed by our Chinese brothers for many years now, on the mammoth sign on the Great Wall at Badaling, 'One World One Dream,' our great union will usher in the peace which has seemed so illusive since the dawn of man's occupation of Mother Earth. Nations and religions will then have no reason to fear one another, for we shall be as one."

Applause radiated, and Julian stood, initiating a standing ovation for the general.

Lorraine continued. "Over the past three weeks a star has arisen which, though stated symbolically, is nevertheless an event which has been awaited by our suffering world for millennia. Each of you has already been introduced to the Gnostic prophecies, which coincide to an uncanny degree with those of Mayan origin, and though no dates were introduced in Hebrew and Christian holy writs, these dynamic prophecies also agree in principle with them as well.

"The young man, whose very name was foretold in the secret Gnostic writings, much the way that the name of Cyrus was foretold by the prophet Isaiah long before he released the Israelites from Babylonian captivity in the sixth century BCE, after the Medes and Persians conquered them, has arrived on the world scene at the precise time which his advent was predicted thousands of years ago, making this prophecy even more striking than that of Cyrus. In much the same way that Cyrus was used by the higher power to release Israel from bondage, Julian will be used to release our modern world from terrorism and slavery to political and religious bondage. And now, without further ado, I give you, the man of the hour, the man for the world, Julian Stuart!"

Tears filled eyes all about the room, as once again Julian arose, and quickly, the audience was standing.

"General Lorraine, highly esteemed members of our team, all of you here. I want to tell you today that all of my life I have felt a special calling. I have known that something lay ahead for me which would change people, and unite others behind a great cause.

"My parents have always treated me like royalty. My true destiny was held back from my knowledge because, in his wisdom, my father knew that it was not my time, and I must be mature enough to accept my rightful destiny. I want to thank each of you, from the bottom of my heart, for all of the dedicated effort which has gone into making sure that world leaders were at a point where the One World Union can now become a reality. None of you will go unrewarded. I have worked closely with General Lorraine and others of you; you know who you are, to ensure that the talks will come off without a hitch. Of course we know that if a problem arises which has gone undetected we have Special Forces which will quietly take care of these matters. Nothing and no one will stand in the way. Let it be written, let it be done."

Jabaldi grinned a wicked grin. He knew that he was just as determined as the opposition.

# Chapter Twelve

The corporate condo in the French Quarter was tidy and exceptionally well-kept. The compact kitchen was stocked with an abundance of Cajun cuisine. A bit off-diet for Klarissa, either for her Kosher Jewish upbringing or her acquired tastes of Americanisms such as pork loin or catfish to which she had adapted after marrying Julian.

Though her family conformed to the basic Jewish food groups, mostly because of frequent visits by her paternal grandmother, they were not so strict that they did not permit "unclean foods" in the house.

She would have loved to ramble through Jackson Square and watch the artists at their craft, or feed the cooing pigeons, but she dared not roam. She felt like a caged kitten.

The last time she had been in the city, the devastation from Katrina had been shocking. At least there had been considerable rebuilding. The Big Easy seemed like her old self.

This was the first time since childhood, however, that she had been on this particular street. As Klarissa entered, vivid visions of bitter-sweet memories which had remained dormant for what seemed a lifetime flooded her being.

All of a sudden she was nine years old. Her mother had taken her on a summer get-away with a girlfriend. The only problem was that the girlfriend had left her with her boy-friend. What had been, up to that point a thrilling trip for just the girls suddenly turned into a nightmare.

Her mother had paid her girlfriend to take her to the beach while she remained behind to indulge in wine and frolicking. Klarissa had done everything to erase the memories, since she had never knowingly been pushed away for further episodes of adulterous activity.

Her mother had never mentioned the incident, but had seemed to sense the toll that it had taken on their relationship, endeavoring thereafter to be the mother to her that she knew she needed; a relationship that was extremely short-lived. Somehow, she had forgiven her and moved on.

Pushing the unpleasant memories aside, she settled on the sofa and aimed the remote at the LCD TV on the wall. The anchor of the evening news was stating the fact that a closed meeting of the One World Alliance had taken place that morning in London. Even at this late date in the scheme of things, the story was brief and fleeting.

At the mere mention of it, however, Klarissa felt the hair on the back of her neck stand out, and haunting chills creep about her spine. *This has some connection to Julian*, she thought, knowing that she must discover how to get to the bottom of it. She dare not call Gloria or Roger, however, for fear that the powers that be had their phones bugged.

"Roger Snowden? This is Mike Montgomery. I'm a friend of Jim Jarvis. I have it on good authority that you are harboring a person of interest in an ongoing investigation by the police in Virginia. Where is she? The police in New Orleans tell me that her car was at your place, and has now turned up in a garage in Baton Rouge. Talk to me."

"Mike, I know you mean Klarissa Stuart. She is an old friend of Gloria's and mine. She did stop by for a visit, but she left yesterday. If I could help, I would. How do I know where she was going? She did ask me if I had seen her husband, and of course, I told her that I hadn't."

"Come on, man. I know that you would be loyal to friends. Spit it out, where did she go?"

"Do you think I would jeopardize a police investigation?"

"I hope you know the consequences if you do."

"Montgomery? Montgomery?"

Roger's honed mind was racing. He would put nothing past this Mike Montgomery. He hit speed dial for the only person who might help him. If he could reach him, maybe he could get to the bottom of things.

"Jordon, this is Roger Snowden. You know that I wouldn't have called you had it not been life or death. This time I fear it's mine.

"A guy claiming to be a policeman named Mike Montgomery says he knows I'm protecting Klarissa. I don't know what's going on. But I think she's in real danger. She was here, but she left. From what I can gather, I feel that Julian is safe. But I can imagine that taking Klarissa out is not the ideal scenario here."

"Stay cool. I'm glad you called me. There's a lot happening here which must be on a need-to-know basis. I'm sorry I can't tell you more than that. You know I care about my daughter-in-law. Do you have any idea where she may have gone?"

Roger hesitated. "She's safe at a condo on Chartres belonging to my mother-in-law."

"Thanks, man. I'll see that she's protected. I know who Mike Montgomery is."

"Montgomery, I've got a 10-20 on Klarissa. Don't, I mean DON'T kill her, but erase Roger Snowden. He could be a problem."

2012: The Awesome King of Destiny          deVere

# Chapter Thirteen

---

"Roger? Are you in there?"

Gloria gently inched the front door open. It was Monday evening. She was shocked to see it ajar. Hastily glancing from side to side, she cautiously began her entry. Since she didn't have access to a handgun, she lifted a small vial of mace from her handbag, holding it as a shield in front of her.

All at once she gasped. Roger's cold form was upright in the chair in his study, a tiny hole in his bloody forehead and a look of horror pasted on his face. Gloria's eyelids flitted, her body went limp. She felt herself blacking out. She grabbed wildly for a chair, but it was too late.

The doorbell startled Klarissa. Who could even know that anyone was there? Swiftly she threw on a housecoat and dashed to the rear door.

The knob was moving! She couldn't bear to think of what might be transpiring. Suddenly her cell phone rang. She could take no chances, so she flipped it off, and reversed her tracks to the front. With one violent kick the front door was open and Klarisa found herself staring into the eyes of a uniformed street cop.

Gloria couldn't fathom why Klarissa had not answered. She knew to stay in the condo, listening for the phone in case there might be some news of Julian. She had bought her a throw-away with an untraceable number, and had the calls forwarded from her regular cell which Julian would have tried, which had been turned off.

It had taken about thirty minutes for Gloria to revive, at which time she had dialed 911 to report Roger's murder. The coroner had arrived to fetch the body for the morgue.

Gloria was exhausted. The first person she had called was Klarissa.

Against her strong attempts to explain that she was not the threat, that someone had been tailing her and was trying to kill her, the policeman still ended up charging her with resisting arrest, taking her to headquarters.

"Lady, I'm only doing my job. No one is ever a threat, everyone is 'innocent,' I read ya. But I was strictly ordered to bring you in

for extradition to Virginia on charges of avoiding arrest in a case of kidnapping."

"Kidnapping? Just who the hell was I
supposed to have kidnapped?"

"Lady, like I told ya, I'm just doin' my
damn job! Don't take it out on me!"

"You're the one who picked me up. I
have a right to one phone call!"

"Yes 'm you've got a right to make one
call."


"Mother, I'm at the first precinct police headquarters in New Orleans. Get somebody down
here to get me out before I'm taken back to
Virginia on false charges. Kidnapping, they tell
me."

"Klarissa, honey, what in God's name
are you talking about?"

"Mother, I told you that Julian had disappeared. I don't know; maybe they've trumped up some charge that I had something to do
with having him abducted! How ridiculous
would that be? I've tried desperately to find
him, and I can't even get him on his iPhone.
Please, and hurry!"

"Time's up, lady!"

Jabaldi tucked his notes safely inside his over-coat and eased himself out into the busy London street. If he had to do it himself, he would stop the Awesome King before it was forever too late.

One of his bugs had let him know that a global conference was being planned for Sunday, May 27, a festive religious high day combining the Christian Day of Pentecost with the Jewish Shavout, the First Trump, or Festival of the First Fruits.

A cleverly disguised attempt to close the gap of differences, he knew. But it didn't work with him. He had drawn a schematic of the area around Westminster Abbey where the meeting would be held. Countless dignitaries would be present, not the least of which would be General Lorraine and their fair-headed "prince." He would get an up-close and personal look at it for himself.

By the time he reached the Abbey, the golden sun was embracing the breathtaking skyline of the city.

*Just as I envisioned*, he thought. *It's perfect. I'll have a ringside seat. I, Germaine Jabaldi, will make history! That cocky Pope Pius XIII will have me to thank. He will realize that I was right! Now I can return to Rome in confidence.*

# Chapter Fourteen

"General Lorraine, Your Royal Highness, distinguished members of the Global Government Committee, as the Paramount Leader of the Peoples Republic of China, as all of you are aware, I have the final word on the official position of our country."

Din Pong, though speaking in Mandarin, was very fluent in English and conversational in most languages being represented. The electronic interpreters were being utilized to make certain that the strictest intent of the General Secretary's speech was coming through to each member.

"As all of you are also aware, due to the excessive amount of funds which our nation contributed during the period of recession which almost crippled the world from 2008 through 2010, and still has great effect on the global economy, the People's Republic has every right to be a major player in the new One World Order.

"In our recent conference with Your Royal Highness, General Lorraine, the UN Secretary General, and most especially, Rabbi Ginsburg, and the World Council of Religious Leaders, who have been the backbone of what shall be an acceptable Spiritual Foundation for our new government, we are most joyous to announce that all are in oneness like at no other time in world history."

As cheers erupted in the Abbey, the standing ovation seemed so natural that it was magnetic, drawing the members to their feet as if by a Universal Force.

The Secretary continued, "It is most fitting that I now submit the floor to the new Religious Czar of the One World Union, Rabbi Abraham Ginsberg!"

"Secretary Pong; Your Highness, Prince Julian; General Lorraine; distinguished members of the One World Order, it is my great pleasure to confirm the fact that there has been a most extraordinary agreement among the leaders of the Global Community, both capitalist and communistic, and an unprecedented union of all religious persuasions.

"I have been accepted as the Spiritual Adviser and moderator for the World Union which shall soon occur. Plans have been approved, and the wheels have been placed in motion, that following the coronation of our new figurehead, His Royal Highness, Prince Julian..." cheers from all over the crowd erupted, causing the Rabbi to pause. "As I was saying, following the coronation, the long-awaited rebuilding of the Temple of Jerusalem shall commence!"

"Alleluia!" Cheers once again quieted his speech.

"It is altogether fitting that our great jubilation would be celebrated on this, the commemoration of the First Trump. To our too-long separate brothers and sisters of the offshoot of Judaism known commonly as the Christian Faith, it is the Day of Pentecost; the day upon which their Church was started. And now, without further fanfare, I present to you HRH, Julian Stuart!"

From his "ringside seat" Cardinal Jabaldi carefully placed the deadly assault rifle in his left hand and against his right shoulder. He had paid a pretty penny to have it hidden there. Nearby, Big Ben began its familiar toll.

"Mr. Secretary, distinguished committee members, honored guests; it is my extreme pleasure to greet you this glorious Sunday morning. It also makes me greatly exuberant to have at my side, my lovely helpmate, Klarissa, and my father, Jordan Stuart. Without these two special individuals in my life, there is no way that I could have the ability to fulfill my sovereign destiny. But they *are* here, as they were also meant to be."

There was a brief pause before Julian continued. "It makes me very sad, however, to announce that my dear mother, Margaret Dupree Stuart, with whom I have been extremely blessed throughout my lifetime, passed away day before yesterday. She will forever be missed by those who knew her and loved her. Her remains were discretely cremated and flown here by special arrangement. We will be holding a memorial service in her honor Tuesday at the Baha'i Temple here in London, on the anniversary of the ascension of Baha'u'llah, for those who wish to attend..."

Jabaldi was constantly plagued by security guards surrounding Julian, and his perpetual stirring about the rostrum. The scope on the rifle must indicate that the shot could not miss.

A rumble spread about the Abbey at the mention of Margaret Stuart's demise.

"But I know that my gracious mother would have wanted me to ascend to the moment. This conference has been planned for some time, and the world must not wait. The hour is short; our time is at hand to go forward with the destiny of mankind. Peace is at our door.

"I have been especially selected for the greatest honor on earth: the honor of guiding humanity into the Utopian New Age. It shall be an age of not only peace, but prosperity, like our race has never imagined. Mother Earth shall bring forth abundance, like it was intended to do. We shall work together in unity to realize the fulfillment of the fondest dreams of humankind. No longer shall the differences of religion, language, national borders, slipping currencies, and greed separate us.

"We will retain a global force to insure that extraterrestrial forces never threaten us. Incidents like that which occurred at Roswell, New Mexico in 1947, and sightings by so many which have been denied by the US and other governments in an effort to keep down pandemonium, shall never again be denied. Our sovereign leadership shall be preserved at all cost for the betterment of mankind, and the preservation of all life on earth.

"No longer shall our world fail to protect our natural environment, and preserve the inhabitants of our planet and its atmosphere which have been facing extinction. Our brothers, the animal and the fish, the wind and the soil, the water and the air, shall have our devotion and promise of preservation."

Applause once again drowned out the prince.

Jabaldi squirmed, and began to panic. Calculatingly he took aim, as his finger squeezed the trigger. The muffled shot zoomed through the ancient Abbey.

# Chapter Fifteen

Klarissa hung up the phone in disgust.

"Come on, Ms. Stuart, you have a car waiting. The chief in Virginia who had you picked up had already dispatched an officer to bring you back."

"But I called my mother to send some-one to bail me out!"

"We have no problem with you here; she can deal with that in Richmond."

"Ms. Stuart, I'm Dave McCoy. I'll be carrying you back for booking. Make yourself comfort-able back there."

"Mr. McCoy, can you just tell me what I'm being charged with?"

"*Officer* McCoy. And my papers say 'avoiding arrest and conspiracy in a kidnap-ping.' "

"And just who am I supposed to have conspired with regarding the kidnapping of whom, pray tell, *Officer*?"

"Ma'am, I'm just the delivery man. I haven't been in Richmond long, but I guess I'm the best they had at the moment. When we get back to Richmond, I'm sure the Chief will fill you in on the details of what you are permitted to know."

"Permitted to know? If the charge is against me, then I have a right to know everything that's been trumped up against me. My husband is a lawyer, and a damn good one. When I find him, you and your chief will be sorry you ever came after me!"

"Find him, huh? Are you telling me that you have no idea where this slick-talking attorney husband of yours is?"

Klarissa didn't bother to answer.

"Good job, McCoy!

"Klarissa Stuart! We finally meet! Did you honestly feel that you could avoid the long arm of the law? I'm Mike Montgomery. Klarissa Stuart, you are under arrest for conspiracy in the disappearance and kidnapping of your husband, Julian Stuart. Anything you say can, and will be used against you in a court of law. You have a right to an attorney..."

"Skip it, Montgomery; you know damn well that I know my rights, and that I can afford an attorney. And I'm also sure you know that I had nothing to do with my husband's disappearance. You likely know where he is, and I demand to talk to my attorney. When my mother…"

"We already have your precious mother. We brought her in for questioning."

Klarissa's blood was reaching the boiling point. "Screw you, you freaking pig! I demand to see my attorney!"

Klarissa suddenly felt a cold hand wrap around one side of her neck, and slowly lost consciousness.

McCoy wrinkled his brow. *I wonder what the real story is here.*

When she awoke, the snug bonds about her wrists and ankles threatened to extinguish the flow of blood. As her sight came and went, she saw her mother beside her.

Their surroundings were obviously the interior of a remarkable airplane. It appeared to be a fabulous Boeing 787 Dreamliner. Their captors had darkened the windows with the mere touch of a button.

From their seats, the ladies were able to view a flat high-def monitor upon which the ceremony underway in Westminster Abbey was unfolding.

The guards surrounding Julian were more than mere security. Mario Angelica, a Special Envoy of the Vatican, had been commissioned by Pius XIII to secretly attend to the wellbeing of Prince Julian.

The close relationship of the Pontiff to Rabbi Ginsburg, and his dedication to the commitment of the Mother Church to the efforts of the World Council of Religious Leaders, compelled him to a higher loyalty than that which he felt to the cardinal.

Especially so now that he believed Jabaldi had gone over the edge of reason in his obsession with futuristic prophecies.

Angelica, himself, had maintained a prominent position on the stage at the Abbey, and had surveyed carefully every possible nook and cranny in which Jabaldi, or any other crackpot, could hide in wait for a window of opportunity to assassinate the prince.

It was obvious to the Holy See that Jabaldi had been absent from his duties and he had discovered that the cardinal had been making unauthorized frequent visits to London.

Binoculars in hand, Angelica spotted the rifle. With the speed of a falcon, he plunged forward, forcing the prince to the floor.

As the shot zoomed forth, Jabaldi realized that his effort was doomed, and bolted from his perch. Downward he spiraled toward the exit.

# Chapter Sixteen

"**D**amn you, Jabaldi! This was never a part of the deal! I curse the day I placed my trust in you! To think, I am responsible for allowing your viewing of the scroll! Now I have to tell you who I am. My name is Margaret Stuart. I'm Julian's mother. No one was ever supposed to get hurt! If anything happens to my husband or my son, you'll have hell to pay!"

"Now calm down, Margaret! I knew who you were all along, but I couldn't risk letting you know that I did. Haven't you been paid well for your services? Didn't they arrive in your numbered Swiss account on schedule?"

"That's not the point! You were only to get the Church behind you in stopping this coronation!

"And whose hair-brained idea was it to have me declared dead? Of course you knew me! You were behind this as well, weren't you? Now I can never see Jordon or Julian again. They must always think I am..."

Margaret Stuart's distinctive voice faded, trailing into uncontrollable sobs.

"Yes, it was my idea, and it was the right one. Goodbye, Margaret. You wouldn't want me to be forced to have you really erased as well, would you?"

Margaret slammed the cordless phone back on the receiver. Her tears turned to a bitter inward resolve for revenge.

She was no dummy, but she loved Jordan and Julian regardless of the farce that had been perpetrated against her.

She *had* borne a son to Jordan. Just after his birth, the child had been taken away by the nurses "for cleaning." When she first held Julian, she had suspected that something was amiss. He had seemed just a bit larger than the boy to whom she had given birth, and his hair, a tad darker.

She had kept telling herself that she was wrong. This *was* her child. How could he not be? She was just dazed by the anesthetic.

A year later, while Jordan was away on business, she had ordered a mitochondrial DNA test which conclusively proved that he was not of her blood. Though she was devastated, she loved him too much to give him up.

Then, before she had had the nerve to confront her husband, she had overheard a phone conversation between Jordan and General Lorraine which gave her no doubt as to the fact that the switch had been intentional. She didn't dare investigate further, for fear of the dire consequences.

She had followed her husband, watching him opening a safe which was hidden behind a large painting in his office. Later, she rambled through Jordan's wallet and found the combination.

Inside the safe, she discovered both the manuscript, and the outline of the plot. She was able to take numerous photos when he was abroad on one of his mysterious jaunts.

Jordan and Julian had both been assured of her sudden death by doctors whom they trusted, who had been paid by Jabaldi with personal funds. They had been told that her body contained a highly contagious infection which made immediate cremation the only viable alternative.

Julian saw this as another sign that his destiny was upon him; that he must now never be forced to face his assumed mother with the truth.

One factor, however, after she had been given time to absorb it, had made the announcement of her passing a possible stroke of fortune. Now she would be free to exist incognito. Perhaps she could finally discover what happened to the son to whom she had actually given birth.

Her marriage had been far from perfect. It was in discovering the origin of Julian that she had learned of Jordan's relationship to Maria de Sancto Claros, the High Priestess. The funds in her Swiss account, totally unbeknownst to Jordan, could comfortably support her diligent search.

She could also certainly wage her own war against Jabaldi. The pope must know. But how could she get through to him? She was dead as Margaret Stuart, and she reckoned now that was for the better.

Pope Pious made the sign of the cross, and chanted a prayer aloud. The chamberlain had just left, informing him of Jabaldi's failed attempt on Julian's life. Angelica had been certain. There could be no doubt. It *was* the cardinal whom he had seen fleeing the Abbey. The binoculars were amply focused. The Pontiff bemoaned his duty. Now there remained only one thing to do. What a shame. What a waste of talent and ability.

"Wildfires continue to rage in Southern California. In spite of dramatic efforts by fire-fighters to control the inferno, the blazes are threatening yet another upscale residential area. Almost a dozen homes have already been consumed. Now in the tenth day, the fire is only about 30% under control.

"Meanwhile, this sad news just out of London. Cardinal Germaine Jabaldi, once in line for consideration to become pope, was arrested and stripped of his authority. He is being charged with the attempt made yester-day on the life of Julian Stuart, a prominent American attorney who is viewed by a large following as a future international political figure. Though the church has faced major challenges in the past two decades due to the scandals regarding sexual improprieties of priests, nothing like this could have been imagined. Can they ever rise above this disparagement?"

It was Saturday, April 26th. Margaret Stuart pushed the off button on her television remote in her room at the New York Palace in Manhattan. This time she had registered as Maggie

Dupree. Why not use her mother's maiden name, she reasoned.

The huge historic grey hotel building, built in 1882 by railroad baron Henry Villard, had been a place of refuge to which her family had often retreated since its day of conversion when wishing to flee their momentary conflicts.

In fact, her great-grandfather Dupree had first been a guest within those thick rock walls when it had been Villard's mansion one Sunday in 1884 after attending mass across the street at St. Patrick's Cathedral.

Margaret sat down on the bed and leaned back on the plush pillows. Now she didn't have to go after Jabaldi. She would find her son. She had pulled in an old marker. His professional position seemed eerily ironic. And he was near. *Very* near.

# Chapter Seventeen

---

Klarissa threw her dainty right hand impetuously over her mouth and let out a shrill screech, followed by a stunned gasp. Having just witnessed a savage attempt upon her husband's life, she could only take solace in the fact that he had somehow been miraculously spared. Maybe there was a God, after all.

"How soon will I be with my husband?"

A scowl and an evil laugh flamed from the face of their unknown attendant.

"For God's sake, tell me where he is, and that he at least knows I'm on the way."

The silence of their captor served as a cruel bender of her gifted mind. Right now, though, being gifted would have seemed a hollow consolation. Klarissa dropped her head.

Her mother reached out, only to be shaken away.

The Dreamliner raced on toward a darkling destination which could only seem to her to be a black hole in the Twilight Zone.

"Gerald, this is Germaine. I've been arrested. I'm at New Scotland Yard. How soon can you get here?"

"My God, Germaine. I just saw a news flash. Is it true?"

"Just hurry."

"I'll be there in thirty minutes." Gerald Houseman hung up the phone and shook his head. *It's a good thing my office is in London*, he thought.

He had attended parochial school with Jabaldi in the 1960s, and they had remained in touch through the years. As their chosen vocations caused them to drift further apart in the ocean of life, they would still enjoy an occasional drink together.

He knew that his old friend had strange notions on occasion, and during their last meeting at a bar in Barcelona, Jabaldi had confided in him a limited framework of his concerns about a mysterious prophecy which he claimed had the potential to greatly undermine the Church.

He had tried to shut it out as a symptom of Jabaldi's personal demons, enraged by the affects of the alcohol, which he feared was the root of the cardinal's far-fetched ideas. Still, he couldn't fathom that one of his eccentric whims could take his brilliant mind this far from common reasoning. He'd have to hear the whole story from the horse's mouth. Or was he now an ass.

The wings of the 787 tilted and the landing gear clicked into place. Klarissa squirmed, knowing that whatever lay in store could only be another nightmare. It seemed that she could only dream of the joyous reunion with Julian that she had been promised.

"Yes. This is the St. James residence. May I help you?"

        "This is Maggie Dupree. I need to speak with Daniel St. James please."

        "This is his wife. What is the nature of your call, if I may be so bold as to ask."

        "I have some information for your husband which is of a personal nature. I know this sounds suspicious, coming from a woman, but I will assure you, it is something I need to discuss with him which has to do with family matters."

        "I am the only family that Daniel has, the fact being that he was an orphan. He even took his surname from the name of the orphanage, for God's sake. What on earth could you be talking about?"

"Mrs. St. James, if you will just allow me to speak with your husband, I'm certain that he will share the information with you."

"Daniel is at the office. He is the District Attorney General, or did you not know that either?"

"Yes, I had heard. An old friend of mine gave me this information which could be of great interest to Daniel, as it was to me."

"Are you trying to tell me that you are claiming some kinship to him? Needing money, perhaps? Well, it isn't going to work. Goodbye, madam, whoever you are."

Margaret hung up the phone. There has to be a way. I'll find him, and he will know the truth.


"How in God's name did you expect to get away with murder? Vigilantes all meet similar ends. Now you are defamed and no one can help you."

"You can."

"And just how the hell do you think I can help you?" Houseman was beyond desperation.

"Oh, I will defend you in court. Maybe insanity will get you time in the asylum rather than the prison. God is the only one who can get hold of your mind and straighten out your craziness, but for that you need faith. Do you even have the slightest touch of that anymore?

"Of course I have faith. What do you think I am? I'm a cardinal! Just hear me out. I'll tell you what you need to do. But you must act quickly. We can still save the world."

Houseman buried his head in his hands and moaned.

# Chapter Eighteen

Gloria d'Angelo sat in the Seventh District Precinct in the East of town begging for clues on the possible identity of Roger's murderer.

She had cooperated fully with all of their questions. It had been weeks with no response. She figured the officers were sucking their thumbs or out looking for women to hook up with.

The goal of the New Orleans Police Department to lead the nation in reduction of violent crime had been making reasonable progress, but to Gloria, it meant nothing. Her Roger was gone, and so was Klarissa. She might be dead too, for all she knew.

"Did ya not have any idea who coulduv done this?" Sergeant Perot asked. A strain of suspicion seemed to permeate from his Cajun voice.

"Not for sure," Gloria said. But I have some ideas as to what may have caused it."

"Oh, yeah? And just what is that?"

"We'd been keeping a friend of ours named Klarissa Stuart whose husband was missing. Jim Jarvis, a guy Roger knew, had told him that we were in great danger if she stayed. We let her go to my mom's condo in the French Quarter. She disappeared around the time that Roger was killed. Check your files. I reported that to one of your officers, too."

"Hmm. And who were you in danger from?"

"I couldn't get anything out of Roger. I tried. I know he was scared."

"Does the name Mike Montgomery mean anything to you?"

"Why? Should it?"

"Well," Perot said, rubbing his chin, "one of the things we check in cases like this is phone records. The last person who called your house was this Montgomery. He called from a personal cell phone out of Richmond, Virginia. Now there's a Police Chief in Richmond by that name, but they usually call from the office. Do ya have any notion why he *could* be the one calling?"

"Hey, Klarissa is from Richmond. Have you had anyone from up there contacting you about her?"

"Naw, but let me call Midtown.

"Chief Franks, Max Perot, Seventh District. How ya makin' it? Did you guys have any action on a Klarissa Stuart in the past six or eight weeks? Oh, is that a fact? You did? Ya don't say. A Chief Montgomery, huh? And a car came and picked her up right after y'all got her there? Didn't ya think that was a little odd, man? And who was the officer who picked the little lady up? Officer Dave McCoy, huh? Thanks, Chief. Thanks a lot."

*Today Venus emerges as the morning star.*

The thought caused goose bumps to run the full length of Jordan's spine as he stared at his 2012 conspicuous event calendar. Venus had not impacted Mercury four days earlier as some had predicted. Jordan was not surprised. *The time will be here soon. The world will never be the same.*

Events had been well-planned far in advance to correspond with special occasions on the calendar. The summer solstice was only ten days away. The meeting of world leaders would occur.

A smirk ran over Jordan's face. Then in six months all would be fulfilled. The Galactic Alignment on December 21st would not signal the end. *The Mayans could only see the problem that would cause the metamorphosis,* Julian thought.

The Pueblo Nation saw the 22nd as the purge and end of the Fourth World, and the 23rd as the beginning of the Fifth World. *What's more important,* Jordan thought, *the Gnostic prophecy states that this year will truly be the beginning of the Age of Completion.*

Jabaldi was roughly shoved into the ARV and locked securely in the back seat. As he stared at the three-sided revolving sign with its plain capitol letters, he almost became hypnotized. Not only by the rapid motion of the sign, but by his irrational reasoning regarding the events which had brought him to 10 Broadway.

"Where are you taking me?"

"You'll see when ya git there, my man."

Jabaldi could merely tell that they were headed south.

The old-world charm of the historic red and white brick Victorian Gothic "Norman Shaw Building" was sorely missed by old-timers. During its construction in 1888, the corpse of a woman, thought to be a victim of the elusive "Jack the Ripper" had been discovered there. This undeniable slice of history had been nonchalantly replaced in 1967 by the plain stainless-steel-clad structure which seemed to bid farewell to the classic image of the mysterious foggy London Streets walked by the mythical Sherlock Holmes.

Mahmud Hemmati could only shake his head in utter disdain. He had contracted to make a hit on Julian Stuart, and this pretentious cardinal had jumped the gun and taken over for him.

Obviously Jabaldi knew nothing of proper protocol in such macabre matters. Now what should he do? Well, he had been cheated out of his thrill. Or should he make the hit now just for the hell of it?

For one thing, he would see that Jabaldi paid the price for cheating him. Maybe the sick cardinal should now become his prey. The fact that he was incarcerated would make no difference to a professional. In fact, it might make it even more challenging.

Hemmati had trained with the best, the elite forces of Al Qaeda. Now that he in the Taliban, he had been largely responsible for multiple killings of American soldiers early in October of 2009 in the rough terrain of Afghanistan. One of his most memorable accomplishments was engineering the partnership between Al Qaeda and the Taliban in January 2010. As a terrorist leader, he had been relocated to London in an effort to keep Britain from committing more soldiers to the War on Terrorism. Luckily, Jabaldi had conferred with an Iranian friend whom he knew had connections to someone who knew how to contact the Taliban.

Hemmati could speak a fair amount of English, and had overheard an American tourist state that everyone in the world is no more that eight contacts away from the Queen of England. He thought the saying likely had merit. He was only two away from her himself.

*Yes, that sounds good to me. The cardinal has committed the "cardinal sin." He tried to take away my thrill. He will pay the supreme price.*

# Chapter Nineteen

---

**P**erot waited for Gloria to leave before immediately running a check on Officer David McCoy. He had been reared in upstate South Carolina in a tiny town that Perot had never heard of, graduated with honors from Clemson University, and then, after a short tour in Iraq, enrolled in the police academy in Greenville.

Perot wondered why he would volunteer for military service when he was a Clemson grad. Then he noticed that he had married the daughter of a colonel in the Air Force.

*Women*, Perot thought, *have a strange sway over moonstruck men. This was likely why he made a decision to continue as a public servant, fighting for law and order*. Perot certainly could empathize.

He had met his girlfriend at the police academy. Candy had been a secretary. Both she and her family were enamored with the bravery which he had demonstrated as an officer by staunchly marching into the face of danger in a hostage situation. *Hell,* he thought,

*I couldn't get out of this job now if I wanted to, unless I gave up my Candy.*

   *It's worth a shot,* Perot told himself. *I'll give him a call at home.*


Meanwhile, Gloria was mulling over what to do on her own. She had tried Klarissa's mom and always received a busy signal. What about Julian's parents? She could give that a shot.

   Fumbling through an old address book, she finally located a number which she hoped would put her in touch.

   "You have reached the Stuart residence. No one is available to take your call at this time. At the sound of the tone, please leave your name and number. We will return your call at our earliest convenience."

   Gloria emitted an exasperated sigh and gave her number with a sense of urgency.

# Chapter Twenty

Hemmati took one last puff on his dingy rolled cigarette before tossing it carelessly on the pavement. He had given the matter of Jabaldi some serious thought. An ever so indiscernible smirk formed on his hardened, callous face.

His rugged features had been distorted by myriads of training missions in the rugged Elburz highlands near the border of northern Iran with Armenia, and his brawny muscles were highly toned. Later, differences in aim had caused him to join forces with the Taliban in their Jihad against the infidels endeavoring to conquer their forces in Afghanistan.

*What had the Taliban to do with the attack on 9 - 11?* he mused, and yet the infidel Yankees were taking a foothold there, and had been for eleven long years, in spite of the torrid rebukes from within their own nation. Maybe now that he had helped bring them together to some extent, their synergy would exact a more fitting revenge.

Even considering the small withdrawal of troops which had begun in July of the previous year, little had changed. *Someday*, he thought, *I will be more dreaded than Bin Laden himself.*

He was now hearing rumors that the prince whom he was to eradicate would be an ally of Allah. *Destiny has a way of preventing disasters and unveiling truth. Allah be praised.* Perhaps he could win favor with the prince, and some day, take his place—one way or another.

Hemmati solidly prided himself with his innate ability to camouflage his true feelings. Why had he allowed himself to adhere to the whim of an infidel cardinal to begin with? *Only as a favor to a friend.*

All was unraveling as it should. He was an accomplished mastermind of terror. Though he had carried forward the teaching and assured his followers that self-destruction in the line of duty was a quick ticket to the fabulous rewards in the next life, he was now a major leader and his services were of much more earthly need. He must survive so that others could learn the righteous path of Islam.

His plans were laid. He would not fail. He would most assuredly bring down justice upon the proper target. Tomorrow would not be too soon.

Margaret Stuart was determined to talk to her true son. Once he was aware of the fact that he had not truly been an orphan but had been deceived and abandoned by one of the most affluent men in America then he would be putty in her hands.

She rapidly glanced at the address. As she was preparing to phone a taxi, she thought about retrieving her voicemail from home. This could be accomplished in but a moment, she reasoned, before leaving, just in case there may be some clue left for Jordon that would facilitate her effort for revenge.

"Good evening, McCoy, may I help you?"

"Officer McCoy, this is Sergeant Max Perot, Seventh District, N'Orl'ans Police Department. How ya doin' this evenin'?"

"Fine, Sergeant. What can I do ya for?"

"I understand that you transported a young lady from down here back to Richmond a few weeks ago, a Ms. Klarissa Stuart?"

"Yes 'ir. I surely did."

"Did you notice anything strange about her, or her case? Is she still in custody there?"

"Yes sir. Well, I don't know what I can tell you. I am sworn to uphold the law, and it was my job to bring the young lady in."

"Well, is she still there?"

"No sir. She was taken away by what I was told were federal agents."

"Federal agents? Just what the *hell* was she charged with?"

"I was told kidnapping and possibly conspiracy."

"How long after you took her in was she hauled away?"

"Same day."

"Again I ask you, did you think there was anything odd about the way she was being treated?"

"Well, sir, I certainly did feel that something wasn't just right. But I was new in my job here, and couldn't buck my boss."

"While you had her in your car, all the way up there, did she say anything that made you think she was being falsely charged?"

"Sir, I don't know you, so how do I know you aren't a lawyer or something? I think I've said too much already. Have a nice day."

Perot cursed. Something was definitely not right here. And he was hell-bent to know what.

# Chapter Twenty-one

---

"**M**rs. Stuart, this is Gloria d'Angelo. I hope you remember me; I'm Roger Snowden's girl in N'Orleans. Roger has been murdered. Klarissa was here, and she has disappeared. I just can't imagine what has happened. I hoped you or somebody could have gotten in touch with me sooner. Please call me as soon as you get this message. 985-555-9856. Please hurry! Something is bad wrong."

"Damn him! Jordon is behind all of this! How could I have been so naive for so long. I'll find out the cause all of this madness if it *really* kills me!"

"Gloria, this is Margaret Stuart. Apparently you hadn't heard that I am also dead."

"Dead? What on earth do you mean?"

"I have been declared deceased in order that I could not interfere with the plans a certain...well, that someone in a place of trust had.

"I can't discuss that right now. I could come out with the truth, but somehow I feel that being dead will serve me well right now. And please don't tell anyone that I spoke with you."

"Margaret, what in the hell is happening? Has the whole world gone mad?"

"It would seem that that would be the case at this moment. What in *hell* is right. This whole mess seems terribly hellish to me. Let me say this, I'm about to meet a young man who may be able to help me get to the bottom of this debacle. I'm in Manhattan. When I know more, I'll get in touch. Is this the best number to reach you?"

"Yes. It's my cell. Actually, after I got back home, I bought one of those new Onyx devices with no buttons. I have it on 24/7. I'll be awaiting your call."

Mahmud Hemmati had hardly rested the night before, anticipating the joy he would receive when Jabaldi was dead.

This was Sunday morning, June 17th. Today was Lailat al-Ma'raj. Today he celebrated al-'Isrā' wal-Mi'rāǧ, the two parts of the journey of the Prophet Mohammed, when he went from Mecca to Al-Haram As-Sharif, the Temple Mount in Jerusalem, and ascended into Janna, the Arabic name for heaven.

What a perfect time to avenge his be-trayer. *This infidel would presume to do the task that only the chosen could accomplish. No wonder he has failed and brought about his own end.*

Hemmati whistled gaily as he show-ered, letting the warmth of the water symbol-ize the sultriness of his soul. Finally he splashed on some smelly French cologne and dressed.

After taking the elevator from his fourth floor suit, he exited through the elegant circu-lar-topped main entrance of the fabulous Duke Hotel in the heart of St. James Place, passing the valet who smiled and nodded.

Making no effort to return the pleasan-try, the assassin hailed the first available cab and spit out his destination.

The cabbie was a happy-go-lucky Afri-can with a pronounced accent, who tried to make casual conversation, which once again fell upon deaf ears. Hemmati was intimately focused on his goal.

Exiting the cab at the corner of Medway with Monck, as the driver glided away, he turned left and stealthily made his way along Monck a mere 160 meters to the entrance of Ashley House.

*They thought they were brilliant, those in-spectors at Scotland Yard, bringing him here. My clandestine connections would astound these "wary inspectors." And* <u>*my*</u> *papers are aptly in order.*

The first floor of the unassuming residence, known as Becket House, was used as a holding center for immigrants with faulty paperwork. The balance of the home is reserved for young people and women who appear to need minimum security, until arrangements are made for permanent housing. One of the women being held on the first floor was an Iranian lady who had not been able to show proper identification, but whom the officers saw as having no danger of terrorism or risk of flight.

"Good morning, Madam. My name is Mohamed Yavari. You have a lady here to whom I am related. I wish to see her, if you please."

"I'm sorry; first you need to show proper identification, and fill out some paperwork, including the name of the inmate and your relationship to her. Then there is a fortnight wait while we verify your request and have it approved by the proper officials."

Hemmati was busily checking the exits, and interior passageways. He had been told that the cardinal was being held in a locked bedroom on the second floor. By this time the attendant's eyes were shifting.

*No time now for formalities.* From his left inside jacket pocket, he flashed out a heavy plastic unknown style air pistol syringe containing a deadly dose of serum, which was injected into the woman instinctively.

As she silently toppled to the floor, Hemmati tore the keys from her side and fumbled for the proper one to gain entrance to the main complex.

Luckily, the other attendants were going busily about their morning duties.

As he topped the stairs at the next level, voices were rapidly upon him. With the agility of a cougar and the strength of a lion, he pounced upon his immediate, unsuspecting prey. Neither the male nor the female attendant had a chance at self-defense. In less than a flash, he had inserted a replacement serum and injected the man then broken the neck of the woman.

*But which room?*

Opening the first door on the eastern wall, he was staring into the face of a beautiful Russian lady. But she looked like no lady. In broken Russian he found himself saying, "kra SAAV eets a. I'll be back for you!"

The next door was ajar. *Not this one.*

Finally he was at the last one. He was almost surprised to find the cardinal kneeling at his bed, crossing himself and mumbling a Hail Mary.

"The Blessed Lady will hear you no more. Unless you really *do* go to meet her."

The serum entered the nape of the cardinal's neck, and he slumped to the bed; then, as in slow motion, tumbled to the floor. Abandoned and defrocked by the church he had vowed to serve, Jabaldi had expired as a martyr.

# Chapter Twenty-two

"**M**r. Houseman, this is Inspector Landau with New Scotland Yard. We have a problem. Cardinal Jabaldi has been murdered. And with him, three of London's finest. And what's more, two women are missing from the facility."

Margaret Stuart's heart beat wildly. She gently stroked her well-dyed deep chestnut hair; meticulously straightened the left collar of her paisley Liz Claiborne jacket and cleared her throat. Every minute detail must be impeccable when she presented herself to Daniel St. James.

The home was a two-story French-style dark red brick executive with an amber shingled roof. Pausing briefly at the door, she exhaled and extended her hand toward the doorbell. Before contact a ferocious Doberman was in her face, his teeth showing in a fashion which could never be mistaken for a smile.

Immediately the porch light ignited, bathing the petrified woman and her unwelcome greeter in a field of brilliance. Momentarily, the door swung open, and a handsome young man stood in its fore.

"Sit, Marky, sit! Hello, how may I help you?"

"Mr. St. James? Are you Daniel St. James?"

"Yes, ma'am. You don't look much like a burglar. Would you like to come in? I should think you'd be more comfortable without Marky breathing down your throat."

"Yes, thank you." *So much for first impresssions.*

The classy heavy wooden door shut in a manner which seemed to speak wealth and warmth in the same breath.

St. James reached out his manicured hand. "You obviously know who I am, and you are?'

"Margaret Stuart. I called to try to make an appointment to speak with you, but I was having a problem communicating my wishes to your wife."

"Who is it, Dan?" Angela St. James was peeping her head out from the family room.

"A Ms. Stuart. Said she spoke to you on the phone?"

"I didn't speak to a Ms. Stuart." Angela was emerging to the entryway.

"I'm sorry," said Daniel "would you like something to drink? Let's all go into the dining area and have a seat."

"That would be great. What do you have?" Margaret asked, following Daniel to the table.

"Allow me to explain, please," she said, turning toward Angela. "On the phone I used the name Maggie Dupree. That was my maiden name, and my family spent a lot of time in New York when I was growing up. Before I'm finished you will understand why I am traveling under that name."

"I believe you said on the phone that your business with my husband was of a family nature, Ms. Stuart. I'll have to admit, given the circumstances, I was a bit leery."

"Would you like something with alcohol?"

"No thanks. Do you just have some ice tea? I want to remain clear-headed. I have quite a story to share with you folks."

"We have some raspberry tea, or we have lemonade and also a pot of fresh Maxwell House." Angela was cooler in her mood.

"The raspberry tea sounds luscious."

"Now, will you please start at the beginning?"

"And that is what happened." Margaret had told them the entire unbelievable story.

Daniel and Angela both glared in wide-eyed wonder at Margaret and looked at each other. It seemed that Daniel was in shock.

"Ms. Stuart, you've told us quite a fantastic yarn. I'm afraid Daniel needs to check out your story. You can't expect us to just buy this tale hook, line and sinker."

"Angela, there's a ring of truth in what she's saying." Daniel pinched his chin between his right thumb and forefinger.

"While I was at the orphanage, there was a nun named Sister Rosa who was very close to me. I can recall that several times she told me that I was a very special child. She said that there was something that I needed to know that she was not permitted to tell me. At times there were presents which she would bring to me. I asked her who they were from, and she told me that an important man had a special interest in me."

"Did you ever see him?" Margaret asked.

"Well, it's possible that I could have. One Sunday afternoon a tall, nicely-dressed gentleman was with Sister Rosa. They were looking at me, and I could tell they were talking about me. When he left he gave me a soft, kind look. It was as if he were speaking to my heart with that look. I just can't explain it."

"Tall. What did he look like?"

"He had sharply defined facial features, and dark, almost black hair."

"You couldn't have described Jordan better. Oh, here. I have a picture of him when he was about your age."

Daniel's eyes froze on the faded portrait. "That's him! Oh, Mother!" His arms encircled Margaret as they wept in unison.

# Chapter Twenty-three

---

Houseman twisted his mouth and cursed under his breath. The cardinal had named him as the only person to notify in case of an emergency. The solitary child of long-deceased parents, the seventy-four-year-old Jabaldi had also appointed his attorney as his sole heir. He would see that the cardinal got a Christian burial. *But I will also find out who did this.*

"Son, I know that your intense training by the OWSC over the past few..."

"The OWSC? I don't believe anyone used that term with me, am I missing something here?"

"Sorry, Julian; that was precisely the point. You're not missing a damn thing. I'm referring to the One World Scientific Committee. They're the tight-knit team of geniuses which was assembled by our top executives to make certain that you lacked nothing in strategic preparedness to become the leader which your destiny demanded.

You were briefed on royal protocol, the extent of your sovereign authority, how this would come into being, etcetera. As the time approaches, we will hold revelation sessions which will introduce each phase of the domination and when it will occur. General Lorraine, Dr. Bilderberger, Dr. Baldwin and I will brief you on a need-to-know basis as these events approach."

"Dr. Bilderberger?"

"Yes. Joshua Bilderberger. He's the distinguished older PHD who shared space with us in Jerusalem in the Nero Palace Bunker. Remember?"

"Of course I remember! But he just introduced himself to me as Dr. Joshua. I recalled him doing a considerable amount of my training during the time before we came over on the Lear. I assume he is of the famous Bilderbergers?"

"Yes. I see you have heard of them."

"I have. In Skull and Crossbones. And Dr. Baldwin...is he the younger doctor who helped with my training?"

"Yes. And there's something else I need to tell you now. You weren't born in Virginia. You were born by cesarean in Jerusalem. Your birth was arranged to occur just prior to Margaret's delivery, then you were flown to the states immediately, and given to her. You have Israeli citizenship papers which have already been cleared with the Prime Minister there. And as a first son through every generation of the Royal lineage of David, of which I have absolute, indisputable proof, you are the rightful heir to the throne of David. When the time comes, you will be declared the true messiah."

"Then I still have a sibling somewhere?"

"Perhaps, but that possibility is of no consequence. There is only one Julian Stuart. Only one heir to the throne of the Completed World."

# Chapter Twenty-four

Margaret and Daniel enjoyed a unique trice of acquainting themselves, one with the other. She dare not tarry too long. She needed this new revelation to sink in after she had left. Margaret was now confident that everything would work for the higher good of all. Not only would she be avenged of the wrong that had been perpetrated upon her, both by Jordan and Jabaldi, but the world would know the truth.

The hush-hush "Gnostic Prophecy" that was becoming self-fulfilled through the efforts of the daring One World Council, would be brought to naught, now that she had Daniel. Once she had deeply embedded within him the ignoble schemes of this satanic lot, he would walk into the midst of the lion's den, if need be, to see righteousness prevail. The Old Testament revisited. It was not that she felt that these perpetrators were of plebian origin, but that their purpose had been hatched in the pits of hell.

At the same moment that Margaret was leaving Daniel's home in Manhattan, far away in Jerusalem, it was early the next morning, Wednesday, June 20th: summer solstice. Jordan was in a special session with the OWSC, the One World Scientific Committee—the core of the One World Council—without Julian or the new Klarissa.

Joshua Bilderberger dominated the podium. His aura was larger than life.

"The Church thinks that their greatest threat comes from science and modern ideologies. They are well aware that these have weakened their position in our educated age. Some are still afraid of terrorist attacks against them. I fear that they are still naïve in their reasoning. Our methods, however, are much more subtle than those archaic tactics for launching revenge upon our enemies.

"We have already rendered them impotent. First, from within, we decayed their principles, and caused scandals among the priests and confusion among the parishioners.

"The world has grown wary and suspicious of those claiming a 'call from God.' They have found that all clergy are mere men and we have made certain that these scandals were widely publicized. United they could have stood, but divided they have fallen. As you know, membership is continuing to decline. We have now convinced those pious leaders to unite with other religions in an effort to gain peace. The lines are hazier than ever in history as to the basic definition of Christianity. Not only the Mother Church has fallen into our hands, but her offshoots are following suit.

"Today the clock begins to tick rapidly toward the Day of Restoration. A lot must transpire during this all-important six month period. You all know what those things are. No one else is so privileged. Even the prince has no need to know every detail yet. The majority of the world has no clue. Today is a great day of celebration. The countdown has begun. Cheers!"

Joshua lifted his glass of water. Tonight the water would be turned into wine.

Meanwhile, Julian and his trophy 'bride' were sailing the Mediterranean in an LSX 75 Lazzara yacht, compliments of the One World Council.

# Chapter Twenty-five

---

"**K**larissa, my love, we've come a long way since we met. Fate has determined that we should be where we are today. I had ambitions that one day I would be widely recognized and respected by the world, but what has happened goes beyond my wildest dreams."

"You are so right, Julian. The same goes doubly for me. All of the time I was worried about you while you were on the run. The anxiety seems so far away now. Wow! We're off the coast of Greece. I've dreamt of the Mediterranean, but it seemed such a fantasy. I didn't think we'd really be here together — at least not for some time. You were always so busy with your practice and all."

The new Klarissa looked dotingly into the face of the prince. She had been born Monique Kay LaRue, the daughter of a French designer, Yves LaRue. A high-ranking member of the True Templars, designing chic clothing served as a front for his truly devious vocation as an international drug kingpin.

Spoiled with all of the luxury that drug cartel fortunes could buy, she had actually cruised the Mediterranean more times than she could remember. In truth, she was a most convincing actor.

Her parents had moved to California when she was five. A prodigy in linguistics, she was already fluent in French and Italian, but she had taken to English like a mermaid to the sea. And she displayed no foreign accent in any of them.

Her height and build were perfect. The Templars had been contemplating the need for an exemplary alternative Klarissa for the past two years. When approached, her family was excited. But she was ecstatic. She would be the queen of the new world.

*What young woman in her right mind could turn this down*, she had thought.

Her parties had gotten boring anyway. Same places, same overheated men wanting to jump her. Now she could have the one man who could give her everything, and she was amply ready for him.

The Templars had the best plastic surgeons in the cosmos on their bulging payroll. It wasn't the first time for such a venture, not by any means, and would not be the last.

They knew the world would be in shock if they were to discover the persons whom they had easily replaced in the past.

"I am so relaxed, Klarissa," Julian said, matching her gaze. This time alone is just what we needed to get those bad vibes out of our system. All those months on the run made me a nervous wreck."

"How well I know. Likewise, I was the one sitting by the phone, not knowing whether you were alive or dead."

The brightness of the sinking red sun over the shimmering water toward the western Cretan coast dazzled their beings.

Tonight they would fully sate themselves. They would sip Leone de Castris Salice Solentino Riserva 2000 and bathe in amorous lovemaking to their hearts' content.

Tomorrow they would dock at the ancient impregnable fortress of Cape Grabusa. An enchanting villa awaited them but a few kilometers from their port.

The real Klarissa, however, was not nearly so felicitous. The 787 had landed in Jerusalem. Klarissa and her panic-stricken mother had been blindfolded and hustled to a waiting

limo; one of those which had served in the pro-
cession from the World Bank in which Julian
and the dream team had been transported.

The ladies were being held in a hoary,
musty rock structure within the Old City. Klarissa was fairly cognizant of the location because of her last conversation with Julian. *That
must have been an eon ago.*

The guards, the ones who delivered the
scanty meals twice daily, appeared to be Arabic, and wielded what seemed to the sheltered
ladies to be machine guns.

They had no inkling as to their origin.
Their swarthy captors were dark in appearance, and most of them sported heavy black
facial hair. Their accents were distinctly Middle-Eastern, though their tongue might as well
have been Greek.

The shifts changed three times a day,
just like clockwork. At night the ladies had
trouble sleeping, because the soldiers, or
whoever they were, stood sentry on the other
side of a thin wall. Having slept during the
day, they would be gambling and cursing
loudly at all hours. Occasionally one would
bring in a woman and have his way with her.

Klarissa and Becky Cline wondered
what might keep the drunken guards from

raping them as well. So far, thank God, they had not tried. Their tiny room was dank and had but one small light bulb dangling on a frayed cord from the musty ceiling.

Klarissa's belly was becoming turgid from weeks of malnutrition. Their desire to have something be done to ameliorate the state of their quarters had only been a fantasy. She thought she must be hallucinating at times. She knew that had Julian known of their locale and circumstances nothing in hell would have prevented his arranging their release. Still, she could not imagine what was, in reality, transpiring.

# Chapter Twenty-six

"Mike Montgomery? This is Sergeant Max Perot down in N'Orleans. How ya doin' today?"

"I'm doing bloody well, I'd say. And yourself?"

Perot paused. *A damned Brit in the Old Dominion?*

"I'm doin' fine, Montgomery. I'm just a bit curious as to what the story is on a young lady that you had brought in there in April from our fair city. A Ms. Klarissa Stuart. I hear she was taken away the same day by federal agents. Can you tell me a little about that?"

"That's a top-secret case, Perot. Where in the bloody hell did you hear that? And just what's your reason for calling me about her, anyhow?"

"I'm working on a high-security case, myself, Montgomery! There was a murder here that I think may tie in with the Stuart lady.

A young computer programmer, who had been trying to help Ms. Stuart, was shot in the head in his own office. It seems that the feds don't know a damn thing about this Klarissa Stuart. Said they didn't pick her up. Now whatcha got to say about that?"

"Could have committed murder, too, huh? Doesn't surprise me any. She was quite a little spitfire."

"You're not listening to me, Montgomery. Or maybe you are, and you're trying to skirt the issue. The feds don't know anything about any Klarissa Stuart. Somebody is trying to pull something on this case, and I'm for darn sure gonna find out who."

"Well, I can't help you, Perot. Shop some other store. Have a bloomin' fine day!"

"Montgomery? Damn it, he hung up on me!" Perot looked around. No one was listening. Only a lonely siren screamed outside.

In her empty apartment Gloria knelt and prayed.

# Chapter Twenty-seven

"Mother...gee it's strange to hear myself call someone that...Mother; I've got to see you again. I've been calling in some favors. I have something for you. Can you meet me at Gilt Restaurant? It's in the Palace Hotel on Madison Avenue."

"I know where it is, Daniel." Margaret's mouth was turning up at the corners. "It's where I'm staying. What time?"

"7:00."

"Will you be alone?"

"Yes, of course. What I have to tell you must stay between the two of us."

Margaret hung up the phone and smiled.

"Yes, Madame, the District Attorney called and reserved a table. He has already arrived. The maitre d' will show you back."

"Hello, Mother." St. James smiled as he glanced up into her solemn eyes. "I got here somewhat early. I thought I'd review the Journal, while I was waiting, to check my stocks."

Daniel rose, and pulled out his mother's chair before she had the chance to do so.

"That's mighty gentlemanly of you, son. They must have taught you *something* right in that damn orphanage."

"Mother! That was my home. I worshiped those nuns. They were my shelter in the storms of childhood."

"I'm sorry, but my sentiment for the Church is at low ebb about now. What's good to eat here?"

"Everything, as you might suspect. Have you not been dining in here during your stay?"

"Only breakfast. I ordered room service for lunch today. But I've just been here a couple of days, and I thought I'd get out of the building and have room to breathe."

"Well, if you really are asking my opinion on the menu, I'm partial to the Dorade Royale. You get Uni Aioli, shellfish, gnocchi, and baby squash."

"I assume they have something I can pronounce on this damn menu. How about something appetizing for land lubbers?"

"Well, they have suckling pig."

"I think I'll look for myself."

"Mother, I was teasing, although they *do* have suckling pig. How about a *succulent* rib eye?"

"Now you are speaking my language."

The waiter was looking down on them when they gazed up. "And what would you folks care to drink?"

"Do you have a good Merlot?"

"But of course, Madame, and for you, Monsieur?"

"I'll be having the Dorade Royale, so I'll require a white, bring me the Chenin Blanc, 1999, s'il vous plait?"

"Oui, Monsieur."

"I really appreciate you, Daniel. You don't know what it means being able to find you after all of these years, knowing that you likely existed out there somewhere, and that I had been deceived and duped by someone who claimed to love me."

"Don't forget, Mother, that I was in a similar position. I thought I was an orphan, for God's sake."

Margaret stared into Daniel's eyes with the acquiescent gaze of a puppy which had just been taken in from Central Park in the dead of winter to a loving home.

Her mind drifted, her emotions still sending shockwaves through her brain. She would hold her questions until after dinner.

# Chapter Twenty-eight

Becky Cline eased to the door and stuck her eye to the dusty keyhole. The primal rays of dawn were peeking over the Damascus Gate. From her knowledge of the Old City, Becky knew that they were in the Muslim Quarter in the northwestern quadrant.

She and Earnest had visited the Dome of the Rock and the al Aqsa Mosque on their last trip to Israel in 2009, only three years earlier. These Muslim holy shrines were to their southwest, *swallowing the hope of the Zionists for a rebuilt Temple to the one true God,* she thought.

Outside, a solitary guard was slumped over in his chair, snoring. There were always two, at a minimum. *Where is his partner?* Becky wondered. Quietly she tiptoed back to Klarissa's cot and tapped her on the shoulder.

"Shhh," she whispered, "There's only one of those guerillas out there. There's nobody else in sight."

"Maybe he took a potty break."

"Yeah, maybe. There's a heavy metal tray over there that they brought our food in last night. If you go to the door and get his attention, I'll stand behind it and clobber him. Maybe God is shining down on us."

"It's worth a try. I'll show him a little skin. Maybe that'll get his attention."

Klarissa tapped on the door.

"Hey! You want some action, soldier?"

The slumbering Arab shook himself and bolted to his feet. Speaking harshly in Arabic, he stuck the key in the hole and turned it till the door was unlocked. Klarissa pulled it open and faced a raised A-91 Russian compact assault rifle.

Unbuttoning the top of her blouse, Klarissa began to back slowly inside, while beckoning sensuously with the index finger of her left hand.

The stench of the approaching guard reflected the flatulent nature of his diet. The Arab's eyelids raised, and the gun lowered as he greedily followed, his eyes glued on the inside of Klarissa's blouse.

Suddenly, as if propelled by the finger of God at Mount Sinai, Becky Cline was upon him, the cast iron tray making swift, direct impact upon his crown. The soldier hit the floor with a thud.

"Let's get the hell out of here!" Klarissa yipped, as she snatched Becky's hand.

As weak as they had felt, a fresh strength seemed to flood their souls. It was the spirit of hope! The visage of 3,000 years of conflict and dreams lay before them. They headed south — directly for the Jewish Quarter. Directly for freedom.

In Crete, a very different Klarissa could never have dreamed that a scenario beyond her wildest imagination was about to materialize.

# Chapter Twenty-nine

It was early Sunday morning, June 24th in Jerusalem. Klarissa and Becky slipped unnoticed along the rear of the age-old buildings.

A startled Arab woman who was exiting her home pulled her khimaar closely about her face and rushed back in. Klarissa suddenly realized that they were in Muslim territory without proper head coverings. They must hasten their pace.

A dirty chicken squawked, and momentarily took limited flight in their fore. Dust flew into Becky's face, causing her to sneeze. Luckily their jaunt was short. They were entering the Jewish Quarter at the base of the Temple Mount! They were able to note the striking difference immediately.

Most buildings were modern structures, comparatively, and very clean since the Jewish Quarter dates only to 1400 AD. Many buildings there had been rebuilt since the Israelis had assumed control in 1967.

It was very fortunate that Becky knew the way along the narrow alleys leading into their safe haven.

"Shalom," Becky said as she approached the friendly wrinkled face of an elderly local lady.

"Alaichem sholom! Arein."

"What did she say?" Klarissa asked.

"She wants us to come in her home."

"I speak English," the kind lady returned.

"Praise be to the God of our fathers!" Becky said, a simper spreading to a grin.

"I thought I would have to teach the entire alefbais to my daughter. She was reared as a native of America with no Yiddish influence, I fear."

"Hurry, we need to get inside. We may have an unwanted apikoros after us."

"You have a problem with an unbeliever?"

"Oh, they believe. They believe that we should be caged like stray dogs. We were being held in the Muslim Quarter by soldiers under the domination of a group who wants us out of the picture."

"May the Lord have mercy!"

"For some reason these Arabs are keeping company with an unlikely lot—the One World Committee."

Klarissa reached out to embrace the kindly woman with whom she already perceived a bond. *Israel!* She felt strangely sentimental in this, the land of her fathers. Yet there was now a brokenness and confusion. Where could she turn?

The kind stranger pushed her back, and their eyes locked.

"God has sent you to me, sister. My son is a leader among Israel. He is a General, and serves in the administration of the Prime Minister!"

"Praised be the Lord!" Becky exclaimed.

Outside there was a clatter of soldiers.

"Quick," the lady said. "Get under the bed!"

"And what is it you have for me, son?" Margaret asked, her brown eyes shifting in anticipation.

"I know where Julian is. And what's even more shocking, I know what Father has done to him, and what he is planning. There is still time. He may yet have hope. And so may the world."

# Chapter Thirty

The hot sunny season was just beginning in Israel. Klarissa was unaccustomed to the dry desert air. Her skin was cracking from lack of bathing and the harsh conditions under which they had been held.

The soldiers had knocked and been sent away with brash warnings relating to the authority of her son. A call had been placed. She and her mother would have an audience with the proper authorities.

*Thank God,* she thought. *We can now find Julian.*

On the other side of the globe, the wheels were beginning to move. Daniel had made a call to his contact.

Gerald Houseman hung up the phone. It was Monday morning, and some sense was coming into this sordid mess. Perhaps Jabaldi had not been as demented as he had seemed.

He and Daniel St. James had met on a Norwegian cruise. A group of top legal minds had formed a friendship through an Internet group known as "Legal Beagles." By way of this tight-knit body the two had become close friends without even laying eyes on one another; until the cruise. Ten of the closest and most affluent of their number had agreed to get together for a time of learning and sharing ideas.

The second common denominator in this group was the fact that they all were bachelors. Ranging in age from 28 to 38, they felt they could share not only in legal matters, but in the very fact that they were all game for romantic adventures which could well develop aboard a "Love Boat." Neither Daniel nor Gerald had been disappointed.

It was while docked at Svolvaer, Lofoten Islands, that Angela first caught Daniel's eye. They had enjoyed a lasting romance over a period of five years, finally culminating in their blissful nuptial.

Gerald had also found the love of his life, Judith Neilson.

Every time Daniel spoke to Gerald, it reminded him of the matchless cruise of the northlands when he had fallen so helplessly in love.

But now Gerald had done him a favor. And consequently, he had done one for his old friend. Together they could find the right combination of contacts to accomplish their goals.

While rummaging through the personal affects left to him, Gerald had found Jabaldi's notes. He had all he needed. And now, so did Daniel and his long-lost mother.

On Tuesday morning, Klarissa and Becky entered the American Embassy. They were pleasantly surprised to be greeted by Yosef ben Canaan, the son of their kind helper.

"Greetings, my friends. 'Tis so good to meet you both!"

"Thank you, kind sir. We did not expect the pleasure of your company, General," Klarissa said, extending her hand.

"Ah, but it is my pleasure! I am no balnes, you might say...uh, miracle-worker, but I will do all in my power to help you."

"We don't expect miracles. Do they happen in our day?"

"The Lord is still the Lord, no?"

"I do not expect him to change. Only times and human beliefs, sir," Becky answered.

"We need guidance, General ben Canaan," Klarissa began. "We believe my husband has been taken into some sort of scheme.

He couldn't know where we are, or how we've been treated."

"What is your husband's name?"

"Julian Stuart. Have you heard of him? We know he came here; then he was taken to England. Do you have any knowledge where he is, or what is going on?"

General ben Canaan felt the blood draining from his face.

"You both better have a seat," he said. "I'm afraid this matter is a little beyond my authority."

Daniel sighed. For the next thirty minutes he enumerated to Margaret Gerald's take on the other side of Jabaldi's story.

He had faked her death to make certain that she would not be questioned in the event that Julian was killed. He related his valiant efforts to triumph through the Church.

He told her how Gerald felt that Jabaldi was *not* insane; how he had gone before the pope to try to stop the One World Union from taking over. Yes, he did drink too much, but he had had only the good of the Church and the future of the world in sight. In Gerald's opinion, Jabaldi had become a martyr for the cause of decent men everywhere.

Yes, he had gotten fanatical, but in his mind, the future depended upon the annihilation of the forces of evil into which Julian had obviously been sucked.

He told her how Julian was now no more than a pawn of the dark side, albeit one that Jabaldi thought was a vital link to the success of the underworld conspiracy to take over the entire global government.

"But most importantly," Daniel said in conclusion, "Julian has been programmed. He's in a constant state of hypnosis. Currently he is en route to London for a meeting with the One World Council to go over the next steps toward his being crowned king. These are the latest facts that Houseman has just been able to find out beyond a shadow of a doubt. He was able to locate the instruments that Jabaldi had been using to track and bug their vehicles. Oh, yes, they have someone with him they are claiming is Klarissa."

# Chapter Thirty-one

The spiffy ebony Mercedes limo came to a smooth stop in front of the stunning Hotel Russell in the heart of historic central London. Monique clasped the hand of the prince and gave him a look of sublime glory.

*With her, what can deter our grandiose future?* In his robotic state of stoic supremacy, the couple was an unflappable force.

As he stepped from the car, Julian tilted his head backward and admired the spectacular brown Victorian structure of the conference center. *Life is grand.* Reaching for the hand of his princess, he pulled her shapely, lanky form outward, and the two followed their escort into the lobby.

The ultra-private room was attended only by staff of the OWSC. The hotel workers were informed that their services were not only unneeded, but that their presence was forbidden.

"¡El mundo es nuestro!" The Spanish Ambassador exclaimed.

The entire group vividly understood the power phrase in all tongues. *The world is ours!* But all had electronic translators as well. Applause resounded through the room and the Ambassador continued. "Soon our money problems will cease, our international boundaries will come down! The world will be one. Each of us will be rulers with great authority!" More applause.

"But now we are gathered for a grand summit, a summit in which we will be informed of our next steps on the road to the ultimate utopia. Señor Lorraine will tell us more."

"Ladies and gentlemen of the One World Committee. This is truly a most auspicious occasion. A day which we will never forget. This is Tuesday, 26 June 2012. Today marks the second standstill of Venus during its retrograde loop. Ik, the Wind, symbolized by the Aztecs as Ehecata, a form of Quetzalcoatl, the great Mayan bird god, which was predicted to come and take his place as ruler, is connected with Venus. On the news this morning, we were informed that worldwide there is a new awareness blowing in like a great and mighty wind. Fresh vanes of thought have been described as such in the past.

"One example was the beginning of the Christian Church, of which it was written that the room was filled with a 'rushing mighty wind.'

"In barely over one month, the Olympic Games will open here in London. These Games are a lasting symbol of the union of athletes from around the globe coming together as in ancient days to compete in a warm and friendly manner.

"Following the Olympics, after the teams have gone back to their respective homelands, an event of astounding magnitude shall take place. This room is off-limits to all but the chosen. Anything revealed in this room cannot be breathed again except in our meetings.

"I know that I will not have to remind any of you about this. The consequences of the smallest infraction of this rule are far too severe to imagine. This will be the first step toward our union and the new leadership taking form as scheduled.

"Many of you are members of our extended family: the holy bloodline which shall rule the world by divine right. The rest of you have been informed, having viewed the scroll which contains the sacred Gnostic prophecy.

"That prophecy tells us the name of the new leader who shall take us into the Utopian completed age; a world in which all shall know peace and prosperity. So too shall this be a world in which there will be no lack of health-care, no homeless, no person which shall lack a decent livelihood. It shall be a world in which all able-bodied men and women shall be employed. In addition, all of our senior citizens shall be granted a fair income, and life expectancy will increase to 150 years and beyond. Is not this secure future worth our confidentiality?" Claps rang out like the waves of high tide.

"This event is inevitable. It would happen at some point in our immediate future. Having shared this, we know how our future must play out; hence, we can time it for the good of all. Many babies currently birthed by the induction of labor, with others via Cesarean section. In addition to preserving life, these methods are also utilized so that timing can be determined. The same is true for this fast approaching Utopian age.

"Our money system has been faulty for many years. Inflation has eroded away the profits, and ponzi schemes have bilked thousands out of their fortunes. Through an organized failure of the banks, as well as a collapse of the currencies of the major nations, it will be possible to bring forth a leader who has the solution. That leader is Julian Stuart. He will locate experts in dealing with these crises.

"He will call on us, and we will introduce a cashless society; one in which all will have access to a common form of currency which will be stored in the World Bank, and will be released through a computer scan. Each person will be given an implant; a computer chip just beneath the surface of their skin. This can easily be inserted in the hand or on the forehead. Having tested these chips for a number of years now, they have proven to be both safe and secure.

"Once the prince has shown the world how simple this solution really is, then he will be proclaimed king of the nations. As we know, all major religions have predicted a new age and a leader who will come forth during such a time. Every country is now ready for a change. Each of you will be a major part of this government! Now, without further ado, I present to you, the man of the hour, Prince Julian!"

Some members of the committee were looking at each other. Their emotions were saliently mixed.

In a plush guest room two floors up, Gerald Houseman was tuned in via Jabaldi's equipment.

# Chapter Thirty-two

---

At the cessation of the conference, Gerald cautiously packed up his equipment in a heavy Samsonite case before casually checking out. The ban had now since been lifted and the members were being served their catered lunch. Enough proof had been garnered. Gerald had a plan of his own.

With the help of General Yosef ben Canaan, Klarissa and Becky had appealed to the Embassy for confirmation of their citizenship, and because of their unique circumstances, had been granted express permission to override government protocol in order to return to America without their original passports.

Upon their arrival at Richmond International, they were eerily greeted by reporters from every major network.

Earnest Cline had made every possible effort to keep their arrival secret, but his endeavors had miserably failed. He had been horrified by the search that had been underway by the FBI for the past ten weeks, and the fact that the story had initially been carried nationwide, and even by the BBC in London.

The 787 Dreamliner flight, of course, had been unscheduled, and listed on the air traffic logs as a humanitarian mission by executives to the Middle East.

"Times like this try the soul."

"Yes, my dear hubby, but God was with us," Becky said with a deep sigh. "I would never wish our experience on anyone, not even Duke."

The sharp-eyed Rottweiler made a shrill yip at the slightest mention of his name.

"Duke has led a very sheltered life for a dog." Ernest smiled broadly.

"Yeah. We should all be so lucky!"

"But now we must find Julian. I just know he's not himself," Klarissa said, frowning. "Could you get the phone, Mother?"

"Better check the caller ID," Ernest said. "All kinds of pranksters are after us now. Especially the paparazzi."

"It's a New York area code—a hotel."

"If it's anything important, they'll leave a message. I'm a little skittish right now. You never know what kind of schmuck might be calling," Earnest said in a firm tone.

It was 10:15, Saturday morning, June 30. Margaret was preparing to check out and head for the airport. She had watched the news late the previous evening with the brief showing Klarissa and her mother arriving in Richmond. She let the phone ring until the voicemail picked up. "Where the hell could they be?" she said aloud.

"Hello, this is someone you know well. The rumors of my death have been greatly exaggerated. But please, don't tell anyone else. I have some news which I need to tell you ASAP, but I can't speak of this on the phone. I'll be in touch when I get back to Virginia."

"Check and see if they left a message," Klarissa said, "just on the off chance that it could be something about Julian."

Becky punched in the number and listened. "I don't know who or what that was. There are a lot of weirdoes out there. It sounded a little like your mother-in-law, but it was likely a prank. Said she wasn't dead."

"Did you save the message?"

"Na, I deleted it, why? Did you want to check it out?"

"I thought I should. We've *got* to find Julian."

"Sorry."

Meanwhile, in London, Julian received a call in his penthouse from General Lorraine. "We have a problem. I assume that you didn't see the news."

# Chapter Thirty-three

---

**K**larissa had dialed back the number on the caller ID and had been told by the clerk that the call to them had been placed by a Maggie Dupree, who had immediately checked out of the hotel. *Something sounds very familiar about that name. Dupree.* But Klarissa pushed any hope to the back of her mind. Her mother had related to her that Margaret was, indeed, dead, and that her ashes had been shipped to London; a fact that made her presume that Julian might still be there. After all, London had been where the attempt on his life had been made, and where the misguided cardinal had been arrested. It was as good a place as any to begin.

"London Chamber of Commerce and Industry. G'day!"

"Ma'am, this is Klarissa Stuart in Richmond, Virginia, USA. I'm trying to locate my husband. Julian Stuart. Do you happen to know if he is in town? He is likely traveling with a group doing publicity tours or something."

"No, madam. We wouldn't know here unless he had been announced on the news. I'm quite certain that nothing has been broadcast."

"How would I know if he were there, in the city, I mean."

"You might try the airlines. They have records of the flights. Or you might try the hotels. This is a big city, you know."

Klarissa hung up. There had to be an easier way.

Margaret caught the first taxi she could find, heading straight for the Cline house. She had the address, but had never been there. "939 Bronson Place. And hurry. There's an extra twenty in it for you if you get me there in thirty minutes!"

"Sheez, lady! What's the freakin' hurry? Your house on fire or somethin'? Keep your pants on. I'll get you there soon enough, and in one piece, too boot."

"I've gone through enough crap. Just keep your eyes on the road and step on it."

"Thanks, cabbie. Here's your fare—and the extra twenty."

Margaret rang the doorbell. Ten seconds passed and she pushed it again.

"Coming!"

The door swung open, and Klarissa stood aghast, the red in her face turning to an immediate stark white. Silence.

"Well, aren't you going to invite me in?"

"I was told you were dead. What happened? Oh, of course, how rude of me, get your butt in here."

Margaret pulled the door shut as she entered. "Like I said in my message, 'the rumors of my death have been greatly exaggerated.'"

*Dupree! But of course! Dupree was Margaret's maiden name! Margaret "Maggie" Dupree!*

"Margaret!" Becky exclaimed with a gasp. "You're alive!"

"Is Ernest around? Let's get past this point. I've got something to tell you."

"No, he's at work. He's fitting someone with glasses, I suppose. At least he tells me that is what he does. He brings home the money, so I don't ask a heck of a lot of questions. Have a seat. Would you like something to drink?"

"I probably need a Long Island Ice Tea, but I'll settle for the straight kind, and make it sweet."

"I hope you bring news of Julian," Klarissa said, impatiently, as Becky went for the tea.

"Yes, and much more."

"We have a story for you, too," Becky was quick to add.

Klarissa and Becky practically held their breath as Margaret related the lengthy account of Jordon's deceitfulness at the birth of their son; candidly outlining everything she had endured, which included Julian's fate, the reasons why she had been declared dead, and concluded with locating her true son, Daniel. The news settled on them as a heavy layer of tumbled boulders.

"I heard about your ordeal on the news. That must have been hell to live through. Tell me all about it."

"Yes, you could say that, but let us have a few moments to digest *this* first. We've got to save Julian from himself," Klarissa moaned.

"There's one other thing you should know," Margaret added. "There is someone with him that they're claiming is you."

# Chapter Thirty-four

$A$t this point, Klarissa was beside herself with ambivalent sensibilities. Her mind ran amuck. How could this have happened? What enigmatical powers could have induced such a trance that Julian could even possibly believe another woman to be his wife?

"Oh God! This can't be happening. After all we've been through, now this?"

"Maybe you'd better lie down," Becky said.

"I'll be alright, Mother, and I *will* find a way to determine what's going on, in order to put a stop to this madness, if it's the last thing I do! So help me, God!"

Gerald Houseman burned inside. It seemed that an undying ember had begun to take over his soul. The man who had been one of his dearest friends since his youth was gone. His feelings had definitely shifted.

Strolling across the floor to his bar, he removed a fresh bottle of Smirnoff Penka Vodka. Opening the bottle, he quickly poured some into a half-filled glass of orange juice. His favorite drink, it was getting more and more difficult to find in the UK. While his great-grandparents had emigrated from Russia to the UK in the 1930s, their descendants had not forgotten this love of the native spirits.

His heritage was looked down upon by many. His father had died young, and his mother was very sickly, requiring constant medical care. Taken in by a Catholic family as a teen, they had also cared for his ailing mother until her passing. They had managed to convert him to Christianity because of their love. As a young man, Jabaldi had been his priest, showing him special attention, making him proud to be a converted Israeli.

When Penka was introduced in 2004, he had fallen in love with its smooth taste. He would continue to find it, whatever it took. The same must also apply to this prince, he reasoned. Jabaldi had given his all, including his life, and now his possessions to Houseman. His killer was yet unknown, but the prince — him he could stop.

Daniel St. James scanned the brief in his hand, but his mind was wandering. The revelations of the last few days were clearly, and loudly, ringing in his brain. Or was that the phone he was hearing?

"Daniel, line one."

"Thanks, Steph. Daniel St. James. May I help you?"

"Hello, son. I'm back in Virginia. Do you have a minute?"

"I'll always have a minute for you, Mother, unless I'm in court, or a meeting, or something life-or-death. How are you?"

"I'm fine, Daniel. Still reeling a bit, but under the circumstances, fine. It's not me I'm concerned about, however. When I got back, I went straight to Klarissa's parents' home. I know you saw on the news what happened to Klarissa and Becky."

"Yes, Mother, so who is it that Julian has with him?"

"That is one of my main concerns. By now they know that their plan has a problem. This has to be on the international news."

"I wonder how they are keeping it from Julian. This has to mean more trouble for Klarissa, and she knows it."

"Maybe you need to send her up here, or somewhere safe."

"She wants to stay here till she has some news. What else did your friend tell you? Can we get in touch with him?"

"I'm a little concerned. He seems to be feeling Jabaldi's mission too much."

"What do you mean?"

"I'm afraid he might go after Julian!"

"My God, no! Surely not that. What's his number?"

It was Thursday afternoon, July 4th. Houseman followed the blinking red dot on the monitor. Julian's limo was pulling away from the motel. Jabaldi's assault rifle was still being held by Scotland Yard, but Houseman had another, perfectly fine weapon; a British 303; an antique from the Second World War with a scope that had been proudly mounted upon its black barrel. The limo was coming his way. He knew where it was headed, and he would be ready. He would not fail.

# Chapter Thirty-five

The sleek Mercedes S Class Luxury Limo came to a smooth halt at the corner of Oxford and North Academy.

From a third-story window in a nearby office building, Gerald Houseman watched Julian emerge first, followed closely by Monique. Taking most careful aim, he firmly squeezed the trigger. He could see Julian tumbling to the pavement. Blood was gushing from his temple. The shot had found its intended mark.

Klarissa had tried to call for the past two days. Houseman was not answering. Since it was Independence Day, she was endeavoring to allow only positive vibes to flow through her consciousness.

She had phoned the State Department to apprise them of her predicament. She was also trying to get the matter to the President. Little did she realize, however, how closely he had been kept updated on it. Now she would wait. It was early morning. She could do nothing on a holiday but relax and be thankful that she was alive.

She had put on a pot of coffee, and the bubbling and hissing had stopped. Ah! The first cup! Nothing could get her going better than that delightful first sip.. Plopping down in her favorite lounger and pressed the remote. An obnoxious car ad presented itself on the screen. So, what else was new? *Ten minutes of commercials and five minutes of show, right?* Suddenly, large words swathed the screen: SPECIAL BULLETIN. A solemn voice began.

"Breaking news out of London. A young man has just been savagely gunned down on the street in front of the American Embassy Passport Office. First reports indicate that the man was an American, possibly an emerging political figure. This rumor, as of yet, however, cannot be confirmed yet. We do know from live reports there that the young man is thought to have been killed instantly. We now go live on the scene to our NBC London Correspondent, George Jenkins. George, what can you tell us at this time?"

"Brandon, the scene here can only be described as surreal. We are told that there was a single shot fired from the direction of an office building across the street. From what little we are able to piece together from several eyewitnesses, the bullet most likely came from a window above ground level. For those of us who lived through the horrible Kennedy assassination in 1964, when the fatal shots were said to have come from a school book depository in downtown Dallas, Texas, I can tell you that this seems all too much like déjà vu to me. While I was only a young child at that time, it's certainly something that I'll never forget."

"Anything yet on the sniper?"

"Sadly, Brandon, nothing. Just a moment," George said, pressing on his earphone. "Wait! There's just been an announcement by the local news. There's going to be an official bulletin from Scotland Yard in a few minutes. They seem to have identified the victim. Yes, they have released his name. An attack was previously made on his life in May at Westminster Abbey.

"There has recently been some confusion because of a high-profile case involving a young lady who was held in Jerusalem, the very individual who was claiming to be his wife. But I'm told now that his wife was at his side. She is being treated at Royal Hospital for shock. His name is or was Julian Stuart."

Klarissa was alone in her apartment. Her eyes closed. She could feel herself entering into a surreal state that she had never before experienced. It was as if she were living the spiraling scene from the classic film, Vertigo. Her phone rang, but she did not hear it.

In a darkened bar in midtown London, Houseman was ordering a Penka and orange juice.

# Chapter Thirty-six

Jovan Stewart clicked the remote and poured a Scotch and soda. Now he knew how Dagobert II felt.

In 469 AD, through a pact between the Catholic Church and Clovis I, in exchange for his conversion to Christianity, the Merovingian lineage was promised perpetual secession to the throne of the Roman Empire.

The line stayed in power for almost 200 years; the last Roman Emperor being Dagobert I. Merovingian King Sigebert III, however, retained limited rule of Austrasia. Upon his death, his five-year-old son, Dagobert II, the rightful heir to the throne, was kidnapped by Grimoald, the Palace Mayor, son of Pipen, who seized the throne for his own son, Childebert.

Compassionately, young Dogobert was spared assassination, and reportedly exiled to Ireland, returning in 679 to reclaim the throne. It had also been proclaimed that the Stewarts were direct descendants of the Merovingians.

But Jovan was determined to prevail. He would stop any revival of a "Pipen the Fat" usurper.

He was a descendant of the other side of the Stuart/Stewart family. When the Morris deed which Julian had been researching had been transferred from the Stewart family, the Masons were also removing something more precious. The property, a stunning plantation, had been the location in which the Gnostic scroll, containing the prophecy, was hidden. Arthur Stewart, Jovan's ancestor, had broken with the Masons because he believed that one of his descendants was to be the promised king, As a result, he wanted control of the scroll. George Stuart had been killed defending this very secret.

As Jabaldi's contact, Jovan had hired Hemmati. While this plan certainly had gone somewhat amuck, it had been a stroke of fortune for Jovan that Houseman had fallen into Jabaldi's passion. The suit over the Morris property had served as a springboard for helping him find the truth.

The family had passed down rumors of a scroll and a prince that would spring from their line. He had seen the scroll. Jovan was closer than Julian to "Jove." Now he saw himself as that prince.

Klarissa could feel a wet cloth on her forehead. Gradually, the geometric shapes in front of her were beginning to converge.

"Easy, hon, you've been out of it for quite a while. How are you feeling?"

"Julian?" Klarissa jolted forward, then laid back, cruel reality sinking in. "Dad. It's good to see you. I guess you've heard."

"Yes, pet. I don't know what to say. You've been through so much!"

"How long have I been unconscious?"

"Judging from the time of the news broadcast on NBC, I'd say over an hour. Mom called me. She thought it would be best if we both came over. I had to finish with my patient and get my secretary to reset the rest of my appointments."

"Hi, Mom. Where were you?"

"I was fixing some hot chocolate when you woke up, but I came as soon as I heard your father talking to you."

"Any word from Washington? I had asked the State Department to get in touch with me about any developments."

"Yes, you did have a call. They left you a message to get back to them. But you'd better get yourself together first."

"But I've got to...oooh, my head!"

"Take it easy," Becky said with a frown. "They will still be there — unless, of course, the world comes to an end." Her tone was obviously facetious.

"Don't talk like that, Mom. The end may be closer than you think the way things are going."

Gloria had tried to call earlier, as well, but the line had been busy. She tried again.

"Stuart residence. May I help you?"

"Uh, this is an old friend of Klarissa's...is she there?"

"May I ask who's calling?"

"Sure. This is Gloria d'Angelo...in New Orleans."

"This is Becky Cline, Klarissa's mother. I appreciate everything you and Roger tried to do for her. Klarissa's a little out of it right now. Maybe she should call you back."

"No, Mom. I want to talk to Gloria. Hand me the phone. Hi, Gloria! It's great to hear from you. I guess you've heard about everything that's happened on the news...."

189

Klarissa's voice cracked and she erupted into streams of tears.

"I guess we'll be widows together," Gloria said as soon as Klarissa began to gain her composure.

"Oh God, what happened? Roger is dead too?"

"Yes, he was shot in the...I can't talk about that yet. I think all of this is somehow connected. I tried to call your cell after he was killed. Shoot, I did everything I could to find out what happened to you! I've even had the cops here investigating how your disappearance and Roger's murder might be connected. I really can't say much on the phone, except that I've taken time off work to deal with this." Gloria paused and let out a puff of air through pursed lips. "Now that I know you're home, and safe, I'm catching the first flight I can get to Richmond. We've got to get to the bottom of this together.

"It will be so great to see you. Let me know the moment you get here and I'll meet you at the airport."

"That may not be a good idea," Becky said, as softly as possible. "Whoever killed Roger and Julian, and had us taken to Jerusalem isn't going to let us rain on their parade."

Little did any of them know that they were dodging an entirely different foe—but one no less determined.

# Chapter Thirty-seven

---

"**W**e have to handle this matter with kid gloves," Joe Franks said. His arms were folded, and though his voice was composed, yet it reflected an obvious sense of urgent sincerity. "The federal government can't take any chances on being involved in a cover-up. Hopefully Watergate taught us something."

"Not to mention Iran-gate and all those other rusty freaking gates."

"This is no time for humorous political backbiting. This is a non-partisan concern which could alter the very future of the entire world," Joe snapped.

The Secretaries of State and Homeland Security, along other top-ranking members of their respective departments were in a hushed meeting at the oval office with the President, who was rubbing his chin.

"We have a definite dilemma here, damn near a national crisis. We have two Klarissa Stuarts, and both are currently in the international news. This is unlike anything we have been trained to handle."

"One thing for sure," the Secretary of State said, "one of them has to be kept silent."

"Damn right," said the President, "and I think we know which one. Joe, as Secretary of Homeland Security, I'm putting you in charge. Do you know anyone you can trust to handle this?"

"I've got a friend with great insight. I think I can trust him. He will know who can handle a matter this delicate."

"Good. Who is he?"

"A District Attorney up in Manhattan, and he's a damn loyal member of our party. In fact, he's working on your reelection campaign as we speak."

Daniel's home phone rang. It had only been five hours since the shooting in London. He was now about to face one of the greatest challenges of his life.

# Chapter Thirty-eight

---

"**H**i, Joe. What's up? It's the freakin' fourth of July, man!"

"Don't you think I know it? We've got a national emergency. Perhaps it might be best if I said we have an *international* emergency."

"Does it have anything to do with the situation in London...the shooting, I mean? That was..." Daniel bit his tongue. Something told him to say no more. "That was certainly a horrible thing to happen. Tell me what you need *me* for."

"Do you recall a lady in the news who was captured and held hostage in Jerusalem?"

Again, Daniel hesitated. "Yes. I heard something about that. Didn't she have something to do with this guy who was shot? "

"It's kinda complicated, but we need to get together. I need your expert advice on what to do. There's a lot at stake for our country."

"This Julian Stuart's been in the news before. It sounded like he had a great future."

"Yeah, you just can't imagine. There's a lot more than meets the eye here. I'm willing to

get together with you down there. In the mean-
time, I want you to put a guard on the Stuart
home down in Richmond. I need to make sure
Klarissa doesn't leave and try to take the law
into her own hands."

"Done. See you tomorrow."

On the other side of the pond, Monique was
drifting in and out of fitful, tormenting sleep.
The hospital had given her a heavy dose of
Valium to calm her down, and later, Lunesta to
make sure she slept, but even a combination of
these potent drugs didn't kill the memory of
the 303 slug ripping through Julian's head.
Nothing could ever erase that vivid scene of
horror.

In a plush penthouse suite, a tall, handsome
young man was looking in the mirror. The face
he saw looking back at him was that of a
prince.

# Chapter Thirty-nine

---

The London sun arose on the hot, dry morning of July 5th. The lingering clouds, which it was hoped might bring at least a fleeting shower, began to gap. Big Ben tolled as if nothing amiss had transpired in his stoic part of the world. A pigeon cooed before swooping down to peck up a meager grain of un-popped popcorn dropped by a theater-goer the previous evening.

Monique yawned. She didn't like it, but she was waking. The Lunesta was beginning to loose its remaining effects.

"G'mornin'," the bouncy twenty-something cockney nurse said. "Und how ur ye this fine mornin'?"

Monique emitted a low groan and turned over to escape the rays streaming between the blinds.

"Ya ain't a-talkin' now, ain't ya?" Turning around she continued. "Ya got comp'ny, now, ya have! So ya might jest as soon get yer lazy arse outta there!"

Monique slowly forced her numb body over, and stared into Jordan's face before reaching up to embrace him. Tears were silently trickling down her unadorned cheeks.

"Get up, young lady. We're in this thing together. Get dressed, if you don't want me to do it for you. I'm taking you out of this place."

"But…"

"No buts. Let's get going."

Monique motioned for Jordon to leave the room, and when he had done so, dutifully dressed. She still didn't feel like doing anything except curling into a fetal position and pulling the covers over her head.

"Where are you taking me? I don't even feel like eating." Monique was putting on her face coat; then making a swipe at her long hair with a brush.

"Let me surprise you."

"Not only is my prince gone, but now I will never be a queen. Believe it or not, I was falling in love with your son."

"Come, now. You're a good actress."

"But I *do* care."

"You *care* for *money*, young lady. I don't give a damn if you don't love him."

"*Did*. Did love him."

197

"You do remember the prophecy. It says he *will* be king."

"Don't tease me about a thing like this. I watched my dream die!'

"You asked where I was taking you. We're about there, and your breakfast is being catered."

"Don't screw with my mind, Jordon!"

The Mercedes pulled up in front of a towering building. Jordon exited, smiling as he took Monique's tiny hand in his. "We're there, my princess. Welcome to your castle."

# Chapter Forty

Jordan knocked on the door with a peculiar pattern. Monique could easily tell that it was a prearranged code. The door swung in, and Monique felt limp. She was staring into the face of Julian!

"But..."

"I warned you that you were getting in trouble with that word."

Julian reached out. The two fell into each other's arms and wept.

"We couldn't tell you. It had to look real. I had to die."

"This is above my head! Prophecies, coming back from the dead. Please tell me I'm not dreaming. You really *are* alive!"

"You're not dreaming. I'm alive. Sit down. We owe you an explanation," Jordon said. "As you know, Julian is a very special person. The world will never know what actually took place. They must think he came back to life. Human cloning began back in the 1990s. Before Dolly the sheep was cloned in 1996, the technology was already in place to

199

clone humans. In fact, as a young child, DNA was taken from Julian for the express purpose of cloning him. The young man who died yesterday was a clone born in 1998. Yes, he looked and acted like the original, but as he grew, we gave him growth hormones to make him mature at double the normal rate so he would appear older. At 14, he was biologically 28. This could also have been slowed, if needed, by injections of our anti-aging serum. The clone, whom we always called Julian, was mentally prepared for his mission.

"When Klarissa escaped, we decided to replace Julian with the clone. This happened while you were asleep. Then, we learned that there might be another eminent attempt on his life. We found a new bug in the Mercedes, the vehicle in which you both always rode. It was like the one the priest had used.

"You know, it was the cardinal who had tried to kill him before. Since we had taken him out of the picture, we knew someone else was after him. We also knew we couldn't take any needless chances on the real Julian getting killed. We couldn't tell you, because the risk was too great. You're a good actor, but you likely wouldn't have reacted as you did when he was shot.

"Forgive us, but it's over. This will work in our favor. Just imagine the reaction when he comes back to life."

"But what about the clone? What happened to the body?"

"Cremated."

"And the killer?"

"We've got that under control too."

# Chapter Forty-one

Houseman blinked and rubbed the sleep from his dark, hollow eyes. It couldn't be time to face yet another day, could it? The clock was a dirty lying piece of gelel. He reached over and switched off the alarm button before managing to arise in slow motion.

On the street below an unfamiliar figure lurked. Houseman felt like he needed another vodka, but the real world demanded a more realistic brew which would allow him to attempt the art of communicating.

After pouring himself a jumbo mug of automatically-perked coffee, Houseman opened the curtains and released the shades. The figure below turned and ambled away, quickly ducking into the alley adjoining his building, in an effort to avoid being seen.

"Klarissa Stuart?"

"Yes?"

"This is Daniel St. James. I'm the District Attorney in Manhattan. I really need to meet you. I'll be in Richmond tomorrow."

"Yes, Daniel. I already knew who you were, professionally, I mean. My mother-in-law has shared with me about your relationship to our family. I think it's great that she found you."

"There's more that I need to relate to you. Could you pick me up at the airport tomorrow, eleven-thirtyish? It would be an honor to take you to lunch."

"The pleasure would be all mine. I'm certain that you've been told what I'm going through."

"Yes, I have. See you tomorrow. I'll be arriving from Dulles on American."

It was Tuesday, July 9th. The scorching sun was beaming down on the black, simmering pavement at Richmond International, forming short shadows, as Klarissa walked Daniel to the airport short-term parking lot. The two only engaged in light conversation while driving to the restaurant, making Klarissa even more apprehensive.

Klarissa dabbed the corners of her mouth with the linen napkin, and rushed her hand to her mouth to muffle a gentle burp.

"Thanks for lunch," she said, trying to mask an unwanted tear. "It was very tasty. And I've really enjoyed meeting you...I just wish circumstances were different."

Daniel could tell that she was still tense about the reason he had called her.

"So do I, but now that we've gotten properly acquainted, I have to tell you why it was so imperative for us to meet at this time."

"I was almost afraid to ask. Please do."

"I really don't know how to begin. I can't imagine what you already suspect. After we talk, I'm going to have to take you into protective custody. When you were captured and taken to Israel, it was partly to protect you."

"Protect me? What the hell are you talking about?" her tears were now flowing in rapid succession. She didn't know whether to try to escape, or be grateful for his concern.

"Please hear me out. I'm the best chance you have for survival. I have another shocker or two, I fear."

"How much more can I take?" Klarissa leaned over the table and sobbed aloud. She could feel the piercing eyes closing in from around her. She felt like the bull's eye of an illuminated target. Surely her life was over. What did anything matter anymore, anyway?

Daniel reached and clasped both of her tender hands in his. The feel was the nearest she had come to her husband's touch in months. A voice within was whispering to her, pleading for her to submit. He was a living, breathing part of Julian; his brother, or at least his father's son.

"Klarissa, I really do care. I was reared under the wing of the Church who taught me love. Right now, that love is flowing out to you. It's the love of God."

"Where is God? Sometimes I wonder if he even exists. How could he let this happen?"

"Klarissa, I don't have the answers to all of the mysteries of the ages, but I do have to tell you that Julian is not dead, and that what he is involved with is bigger than all of us."

Klarissa stared blankly out the window of the Strawberry Street Café. A chilling wave of goose bumps ran over her like oil from a giant decanter. "Just take me. May I place a call to my mother?"

"Yes, but make it brief. Just tell her you're going to have to be out of town for a while, that you have gotten some information on what happened to Julian, and you're not sure when you can get back to her."

# Chapter Forty-two

---

It was Sunday, August 5th, and the London Olympic Games were nearing their glorious conclusion. It was the celebration in the Christian world of the transfiguration: the appearance of Jesus in the resurrected body to select disciples. The stage was being set. The next phase was ready to be played out.

The London Times had been printing all night. They had pulled the headlines, taking the time to redo the front page at 10:00 PM. The new, unprecedented headline read, "JULIAN STUART IS ALIVE!!!"

The news spread like wildfire around the globe. Every network ran it as their lead story. The preposterous article claimed that Julian had been pronounced dead on the scene of the shooting, and that his fatal wound had healed while lying in the mortuary.

It further stated that a cremation was reported until Julian could confer with his political associates and decide how to make the announcement.

The story said that Julian had presented himself to the British Royal family at Buckingham Palace, and, with a statement by his personal physician, who had flown in from Virginia, had proven without doubt that it was really he who stood before them, completely well and in excellent physical condition.

What was even more remarkable, there was no scar that remained from the bullet which had torn open his skull. A side headline announced that the pope had declared the event a miracle, and there had even been talk of a possible sainthood.

By now, Klarissa knew that she had made the proper decision in allowing her brother-in-law to place her into protective custody. She was registered under an alias at a secret, secure facility for battered women. Battered! She had certainly felt the part, despite the fact that the familiar usage of the home was for women who had been or were being abused by their husbands or live-in boyfriends.

Given the unique nature of her case, she had been granted a private room. The news reports were still saying that she was at Julian's side. Since she had been back in Richmond, however, she had barely been outside of home;

either hers and Julian's, or the one belonging to her parents.

In the brief call that she had made to her mother, she had instructed her to contact Gloria on the premise that she would be away because of the news which she had received regarding Julian. In light of this, there had been no ripples in the proverbial pond. She reasoned that everyone would now believe that she was truly at his side.

Houseman ducked into a cutlery shop on Cavendish Place. Someone was following him. No one would expect to find him browsing in there, he thought. After asking the salesman some off-the-cuff questions about the knives and their individual uses, he slipped out again, edging his way eastward along Margaret Street toward home. *For now I have lost the bastard*, he thought.

It was in rounding the final corner that he felt his arm being jerked. The sinking needle of a silent syringe was the last sensation he experienced as he slumped into the arms of Mahmud Hemmati.

# Chapter Forty-three

DOLLAR FAILS CAUSING CURRENCY CRASH AROUND THE WORLD. It was Monday, August 27th, exactly 2520 days (7 x 360, eerily, the precise length of the biblical "Great Tribulation") after the annular solar eclipse on Rosh Ha'shanah, October 3-4, 2005. The headline on USA Today was echoed by every newspaper in America, firstly, followed by the rest of the world. Black Monday was a term first coined in Dublin Ireland on Easter Monday, 1209. A group of five hundred recent settlers from Bristol had been massacred by Gaelic warriors of the O'Bryne Clan. Several other Mondays since have also been placed in this category, but in modern terms, the stock market crash of Monday, 28 October 1929, had defined the term in the most explicit manner ever. A new standard had been set, in that none had ever come close. This was to be the Black Monday to end all Black Mondays.

Conditions worldwide resembled the demonstrations in Cairo in early 2011. Multifarious riots had broken out. In Chicago, the

Sears Tower had been rashly vandalized, and then set ablaze. Grocery stores around the world were being broken into. Every national leader had declared a state of emergency. The only nations which had not yet been grossly affected were third-world countries. In Jerusalem, many were forsaking all and fleeing to Petra.

Ernest and Becky Cline were thankful for the extra non-perishables that they had stored in their basement. They barred their doors. Phones and electrical power failures were widespread.

Margaret used her BlackBerry to send a text to Daniel, who then invited her to join them in Manhattan. Luckily, she had a hybrid with a full tank. As she drove, she found moving a near impossibility. Traffic was jammed everywhere. She turned on the radio, only to discover that regular stations had ceased to transmit. Finally, she stopped the dial on the emergency frequency.

"Rumors are circulating that the end of the world is upon us. Not only have all the global money systems collapsed, but there are several reports that the most horrid earthquakes in recorded history are likely within the next few weeks, or quite possibly days. Conspiracy theorists are saying, 'we told you so, and you wouldn't listen.' Many are claiming that this was predicted in this or that prophecy. Some are expecting the arrival of Quetzalcoatl; some, the second coming of Jesus. Others are predicting an alien invasion."

Cold chills ran down Margaret's spine. *Maybe there is something to all this prophecy stuff.*

Margaret was stalled in bumper-to-bumper traffic. Horns sang out their soulful cries for help. Darkness was approaching, and she was not even half way to her destination.

Daniel, knowing that a text would be useless, dialed Margaret's cell number. The clamor about her was so deafening that the musical ring was almost muted. Luckily, just as he was about to give up, she answered.

"Where are you, Mother? You should have been here hours ago."

"You wouldn't believe me."

"Try me."

"I'm barely into Jersey. I just crossed The Delaware."

"Be careful. There's lots of looting and carjacking going on."

"You can be sure I'm doing my best. If I'm not there in three hours, send the National Guard after me."

"That may not be a joke."

"Don't talk like that, son."

In London, a party was in progress. The One World Council was preparing to make a crucial announcement.

# Chapter Forty-four

Television cameras from BBC zoomed in on the dynamic speaker. The ears of the entire world were eagerly awaiting every word yet to come. All possible and available networks had taken the feed.

"The global situation has rapidly deteriorated. As you know by now, the governments of the major powers have issued vouchers and debit-type cards which are being accepted as legal tender until a permanent solution is implemented. The world must continue to survive.

"All major airports, which have been shut down for days, have now reopened and are on immediate alert. Strict screening of all international flights between countries will require pat-downs and full-body scans of each and every passenger.

"A somber cry is rising for a charismatic leader to resolve the problems which perplex us all, and threaten to annihilate our race. That leader is in our midst today, and a new date has been set for his coronation by our core team.

It is a date which was always in our plans as the best alternate, should the need be deemed a pressing one. It was on 17 September 1595 that Pope Clemens VII recognized Henri IV, an ancestor of Prince Julian, as king. On this date in 1678, France and Spain signed a peace treaty. It was also on this date in 1745 when the Jacobites under the Young Pretender, Bonnie Prince Charlie, of this same royal Stuart Dynasty, occupied Edinburg. And on 17 September 1778, the first treaty was signed between the new nation, the United States of America, and the natives at Fort Pitt, Pennsylvania, and then, nine years later to this very day, the US Constitution was adopted at Philadelphia. And in more recent history, the North Atlantic Treaty Council met for the first time on 17 September 1949.

"So you see, ladies and gentlemen, destiny has once again brought us to the preordained occasion that must occur for the betterment of all of mankind. Please lift your glasses with me in a toast to the savior of the day, a man highly respected by both major candidates for US president, His Royal Highness, Prince Julian Stuart!"

Julian stood and gracefully bowed, his searching eyes examining the sea of subjects-to-be before him. His finest day was rapidly dawning. Cheers cascaded from every level of the center, like surround sound within a refined cinema.

Lorraine smiled broadly as he gently lowered his Stoelzel crystal stem and placed the goblet to his lips. On the same stage, Bilderberger's thoughts were highly dancing. *Le monde est le mien. Prince, indeed!*

Across the Atlantic, Jovan Stewart was at Norfolk International going through a security patdown. But his brain was in overdrive. He was making plans of his own. Time was closing in as a weighty curtain on the play of the ages.

# Chapter Forty-five

---

Daniel sighed deeply as Margaret's car pulled into his drive. It seemed that even Marky was glad to see her. Not showing her teeth was a good sign. Angela even greeted her with amicable openness, and not the sneering mannerism which she had exhibited at Margaret's first visit.

Klarissa was adapting and still biding her time. Daniel informed Margaret of his plan for her. Margaret understood. Klarissa only deserved the best; she had played no part in the tangled scheme of deception which had quickly eroded her life.

Jovan knew that he had been fortunate to be flying at all. Airlines were at a near shut down, but his connections had never failed him. Feeling the jet begin its descent toward Heathrow, he blinked his eyes and yawned. Having seen the movie before, he had removed the headphones, eagerly reclining his seat for the three hours which followed.

Normally he didn't sleep well in flight. Since he was able to do so, he felt that he must have been wearier than he had thought. He clicked his jaws in a near-futile attempt to curtail the rush of fluids to his ears. Knowing that he hadn't been plagued with this problem for quite a while, he was angry that it was coming on him at this crucial time.

Having just celebrated his thirtieth birthday on July 31st, Jovan had a distinctive "driver" or "red" personality. Reared in the Tidewater area, he had spent his college years in the UK at the famed eight-hundred-year-old University of Cambridge. Discovering his rightful place as heir to the dynasty which had been stolen from him had been the zenith of his experiences. Unlike Julian, he had always craved power with a vengeance.

In his London speech, Julian had announced that the world summit was slated for the next Wednesday, September 5th. The sands of time would flow rapidly. All the worldly heads of state would be present. This date was no accident either. It had been planned to coincide with the date associated with the return of Quetzalcoatl.

The day arrived. Every possible snag had been anticipated and untangled, except the advent of Jovan Stewart.

Joshua Bilderberger stood, his very presence invoking both respect and an aura of awe. He was known, yet unknown. The richest man in the world, his fortunes were uncharted and his power unrealized, not only by the world at large, but even by those who felt that they knew him best. The fact was...no one *really* knew him.

As a child, Joshua was closely tutored by his magisterial mother. His future was to be of no less import than a god. As a member of the elite underground, both families, maternal and paternal, were masters of fate. It was in him, henceforth, that the rivers of destiny had merged.

It was he, and he alone, who had decided that Julian would hold the position in which he was being perceived. It was from his mother's family that the manuscript had been passed for safekeeping to the True Templars when they had initially journeyed to the new world, long before Columbus. It had been through the Illuminati that the secrets of world domination had been passed down from the time of the Merovingians. The Illuminati had infiltrated the Masons, risen to the higher ranks and unbeknownst to the average member, had formed the course of history.

He was Caesar; Julian was Herod. But no one must suspect the spring from which the force erupted; at least not yet.

Joshua lifted his arms even with his slender waist, extending them slightly to both sides. The crowd seemed mesmerized in his presence. The hush was mystical.

"Ladies and gentlemen, my name is Dr. Joshua Bilderberger. It is my distinct honor to address this most distinguished body on this day of days. By way of the web conferences which piloted us here, today will only be a confirmation of the agreed-upon terms which unite our globe and bring us to the precipice of the Utopian age, an age which has only existed in the minds of man heretofore.

"The vast difference between the new world system and the mega-kingdoms of distant history is that our world has come together out of need and desire for unity, and not because of fought-for military victories. The recent wars which have been going on over power and oil, and which escalated during the past decade between the East and the West, the Muslims and the Christians, and which have embattled and endangered the Middle East to no end, have now concluded by agreement rather than conquering an enemy.

"We have all become allies by determining that all can share in the leadership under a common government. We shall now enter our New Age of enlightenment with oneness of mind and goals. Under this agreement, the insightful visions of great minds of the past will finally be realized. Carl Marx, the often misunderstood genius and father of Communism, only wanted what was originally a principle of Christianity. 'From each according to his ability, to each according to his need' is the core goal of our New World System.

"No longer will millions have to die of starvation for lack of food. Under our new system there shall be plenty for all. Prince Julian Stuart, soon to be our leader…"

Waves of applause began erupting, and the leaders all began popping to their feet.

"Please, ladies and gentlemen, allow me to continue. Prince Julian has been a leading member of the committee which has drafted the Constitution, to be approved today as a matter of record, which with his leadership will govern our world. By way of this historic government, one which will combine the visions of great men and women of history, we will no longer have need for paper and coin currencies of the past.

"As you all know, theft and crime will be unnecessary. Each person will have an account with the One World Bank, and will receive a tiny chip implant. Each computer and Internet-ready phone will be equipped with scanners which will determine the available funds in each person's account. While we have had this capability for a considerable time, it is now ready to become the reality. Clinics in every city with a population of 15,000 or more will soon be set up. Each person will be given instructions as to when to report for implantation based on their surname.

"No longer will we need to be concerned about healthcare. Differences like those which have long divided the Americans, and which caused angst between the political factions in America in 2010, shall haunt us no more. Each individual will be assigned physicians and treatment centers. Annual physicals will aid in detection of viruses and diseases.

"No longer will we need to be concerned about illegal drugs; all drugs will be legal and controlled by the World Food and Drug Administration. No longer will we be concerned about prostitution. This too will be legal and government controlled.

"A One World religious board will make available services to those who still feel the need for Spirituality. The value of inner peace and guidance will be emphasized.

"Before you we have placed copies of the new Constitution for your ratification. Now, without further ado, I present to you, the man soon to lead our great world as it has never been led before, His Royal Highness Julian Stuart."

The crowd of dignitaries was on their feet before Julian reached the podium.

"Please, ladies and gentlemen, am I not a man and the son of man? I truly tell you, I am most humbled by your gracious welcome, despite the fact that until of late, the world knew naught of my existence.

"I am most indebted to the One World Council, and the One World Scientific Committee, and their most illustrious leaders, Dr. Joshua Bilderberger, Divisional General Seton Lorraine, Surgeon General, Dr. Randall Baldwin, Rabbi Abraham Ginsberg and my noble father, Dr. Jordan Stuart. My father may rightly be referred to as 'Doctor' because of his LLD.

"Each of these gentlemen has worked tirelessly to assure that the transition of power be accomplished properly and smoothly, and that the leaders of each and every country be considered. I worked with each of them in drafting the new Constitution. I am also deeply appreciative of all of you, my associates, in your understanding and undying commitment toward peace. You will not go unrewarded. As your Commander and Chief, my door will always be open to your concerns, both figuratively and literally. In less than two weeks our dream will become the reality.

"The ancient Hopi nation, natives of the American Southwest, similar to the Mayans, saw the great change as coming this year. According to these immensely advanced and spiritually-tuned peoples, 21 December was not to be the end of the world, but merely the culmination of the present age as well as the beginning of the new, advanced age.

"The Galactic alignment, which was brought to modern awareness only a short time ago, a fact that many saw as connected to the Mayan calendar, has already occurred. The great European astronomer, Jean Meeus, and author John Major Jenkins were right. But the era of awareness is just dawning. Now is the time to reveal, to uncover to all intelligent peoples — those who are to ride the wave with us into the exciting new age — the fact that through the advancements of science, the effect of this alignment is changing the minds of mankind.

Though my coronation is to occur slightly earlier than originally designated, it is working for the better, because by the winter solstice, which is truly a symbol of that glorious age, all will be in order. The new system will actually be activated upon that very date!"

Applause erupted. In the back of the auditorium, Jovan gritted his teeth. *Did they think that world politics would be any different with this new change? Did they not imagine any competition?*

# Chapter Forty-six

---

Monday morning, September 17th, had finally dawned. Thousands had thronged to London from every corner of the earth. Big Ben's distinctive cry echoed eight reverberating times throughout the ardent city. Next door, the organ was wailing softly as the Coronation of King Julian was about to get underway at the incomparable Westminster Abbey. The British royal family, in all of their finery, properly seated on the stage, had been assured that in no way was their throne in jeopardy. Each male member retained his place in line as the figurative monarch of the United Kingdom. Likewise with the prime minister, nothing would be altered. They would merely operate under the auspices of the One World Union. Every nation's government would continue to precede much as before. They would simply possess more assurance of international oneness with the other nations.

Julian had spent the previous evening with the chief of Clan Stuart of Bute; Lord Lyon, King of Arms; some prominent earls, and other dignitaries of Scottish peerage. He was impressed with the need for unity among these factions.

Over the past weeks, Daniel had used every conceivable means to get through to his brother, but each call had been cleverly blocked. Now he had arrived in London, and though he had failed to stop the coronation he was determined to contact the woman parading as Klarissa. He had arranged with the Presidential staff to attend the ceremony as a member of the official American entourage. Everyone who was anyone of status was there. Though security was at immediate alert, no one had any reason to question him in any respect.

Jovan had not been so fortunate. He must make his own luck. Fortunately, he was a master of doing so. As he sat in the mysterious, ancient Abbey, his mind rehashed the obtaining of his needed legal papers.

Upon arriving in the city he had immediately made contact with the underground document forgers.

"Greetings, my friend. We meet again. I need the most current British ID. Passport, driver's license, and all that crap. Make it in the name Jacob Sterling. How soon can I pick them up?"

"I'll have them this afternoon. Our methods are quite effective."

"Oh. Yes. And I need to have a legit invitation to the coronation on Monday."

"That, my friend, will cost you dearly."

"How much?"

"Five thousand pounds. Your total bill is six thousand."

"No problem. See you about 5:00."

Since the 1911 coronation of George V, the Abbey had been able to seat 8,000 persons. For this coronation many requests for admission had been turned away. Only the world leaders, the elite crust of society, and privileged press could gain admittance.

As Julian awaited his magical moment, between pleasantries, the vivid memories of his attempted assassination in this place by Cardinal Jabaldi rang in his head. He shook himself as the shrill of the shot seemed to rip through his brain. It had been far too close a call. He had been fortunate that the subsequent reenactment by Houseman had been detected, and yet he felt incredible sadness at knowing that the clone taking the fall for him. Should he be feeling sorrow for this unfamiliar clone? *Destiny,* he reasoned. *No one can alter it. The prophecy must now be fulfilled.*

# Chapter Forty-seven

---

By Julian's side sat the stunning figure of Monique, all that Klarissa had ever been, and more; sexy, vibrant, and famished for the power that awaited her. *If only he knew the truth.* The words formed solidly in her mind as clearly as if they had escaped her sleek, lovely lips. She raised her angel-like eyes, and Julian, seeming to feel them, lowered his own to greet them.

The Duke of Windsor arose. The din of the crowd subsided as in stages, and a reverent hush moved in to replace it.

"Honorable Prince, Your Holiness, distinguished world leaders and most honored guests. Today there is assembled in this chapel perhaps the largest and most high-ranking group of individuals ever brought together in one place at one time, in the history of our civilization. In fact, there has never been a more hallowed occasion. It is my most distinct pleasure to have been asked by Dr. Joshua Bilderberger to open this most especial of ceremonies. With this day a new world is mounting on the horizon. One in which we need have no fear of the archaic differences which have separated and alienated us from one another as nations and members of the human race.

"In a brief moment, our master of ceremonies will stand before us all and have the distinct honor of crowning the predestined king of our race. Under his capable leadership, each of you will hold a position of dignity among each other, having the respect of the entire world.

"I know that I do not have to remind you that Prince Julian was recently gunned down in the streets of our fair city and that his miraculous return to life sent shockwaves around the globe. My family and I have felt nothing but goodwill from him. He has been hailed by all major religious heads as the un-disputed savior of mankind. Having been nominated for sainthood by the Roman Church, he has also been hailed as the awaited messiah by the nation of Israel, the country of his birth. He holds dual citizenship in both Israel and the US, and has now been offered complete honorary British citizenship as well, because Scotland is the native home of his direct male dynastic lineage. Now recognized in Berks Peerage as the heir to many thrones, he is also being referred to as 'The Awesome King of Destiny' by his past critics. As he is welcomed here by my family, so, too, is there deep certainty that he is loved and needed here, in the hearts of mankind as the harbinger for peace everywhere.

"It is now my utmost pleasure to give you, most distinguished leaders and guests, the master of ceremonies for this momentous occasion, Dr. Joshua Bilderberger!"

Amid peels of acclamation, Joshua stood. As he did, the applause grew to a deafening clamor.

"Please, please! Thank you! Thank you! It's difficult for me to express what I feel. Ladies and gentlemen, while I deeply appreciate your exuberance, I am not the man of the hour. I am merely here to echo the words of the Duke of Windsor. As he has already eloquently stated, we are here today to honor the man who has been recognized not only for the genius that he possesses, but also for who he *really* is.

"I can never say enough about this extraordinary man. In the past several months I have gotten to know this exceptional individual as only a select few have known him. Without a doubt he has the tenacity, the mindset, the wisdom, and even the maturity to make the crucial decisions needed to rule over the nations. Likewise, so, too, he is able, when necessary, to seek additional expert advice. I want him to know that I will always be there for him. *He has no idea.*

"Though I could elaborate in my undying confidence and praise of Prince Julian, further statements are unneeded. A unique crown has been crafted by Jacobi and Cone, official jewelers of the One World Scientific Committee. This crown contains the bejeweled lion of the tribe of Judah, in which the king-designate has his roots, as well as the golden serpent of the tribe of Dan, also among his ancient forebears. May I have the crown, please?"

As Lorraine was handing him the crown, a stranger arose from within the pews and began to make his way down the aisle toward the podium. Every eye was upon him.

# Chapter Forty-eight

---

Mario Angelica had certainly not forgotten
the memory of that previous horrific episode
within these very historic walls. With instincts
that were trained to respond accordingly, his
gun flew silently into position.

As the figure continued to proceed forward, no one dared to breathe too heavily. Security personnel moved in like the creeping
spirits of saints of eons past. When the hands
of the stranger slowly crept above his head
there were many collective sighs that could be
heard, while others seemed to remain in sus-
pended animation.

"I am here, Dr. Bilderberger, Your Highness, and Your Holiness, distinguished leaders,
to reveal to you the truth. I am the rightful heir
to this throne. My name is Jovan Stewart.
S-t-e-w-a-r-t. The man before you is an impos-
ter. I have proof of this in my pocket..."

"Please, sir, whoever you may be is im-
material," Joshua said in a crisp, firm tone.
"Prince Julian is being crowned forthwith. This
is no time for such an unwanted intrusion.

"Officers, take this man into custody." Bilderberger's heart pounded wildly. He knew too well who Jovan was, and he must be stopped.

The royal guards closed in with one grabbing Jovan by his right wrist. Jovan jerked, immediately flinging his fist at his would-be captor. On the other side, another guard tackled him, forcing him to the floor. Shocked gasps filled the Abbey. Handcuffs were quickly on his wrists before the guards turned him over to three bobbies, who then led him away and out of the Abbey.

"This is *not* over! Dagobert will be avenged!" Jovan shrieked.

As the bobbies exited, Daniel noticed another striking figure flanking them quietly, assuring safe passage. *Could it be? Was this his old classmate from college?* Obviously he had considerable clout in this situation. The right sleeve of his uniform bore the pyramid capped with the all-seeing eye—the unmistakable insignia of leadership in the OWSC! Yes...it was him!

Mutely Daniel arose and followed, knowing that he must arouse no suspicion. Veering toward the men's room, he ducked into an alcove, whereby he could bide his time.

*He will likely return the same way he left.* Daniel's hope was soon rewarded.

"Mario!"

The stunning officer spun to stare into the face of his old classmate.

Mario Angelica now had carte blanche with the OWSC. Not only was he the Captain of Security, but he was the only council member with such lofty status. His solid connections at the Vatican were also a huge plus. In the event of his death, his sealed files and unlimited perks would pass to the next highest ranking member of the security team, et al.

Angelica's facial muscles, hardened from instinct, reverted to their normal softness.

"Buen giomo, mio amico! How are you a part of this glorious event?"

"It's a long story. Of course your presence here is just as unexpected to me."

"I have no time to talk now, I'm on duty to His Royal Highness, but I would be delighted to invite you to my home… perhaps for dinner? How long will you be in London?"

"I have an open Visa, as I was unsure of the time my mission would entail."

"Mission? Sounds misterioso. Better for later…tomorrow evening then, 7:00? Are you alone?"

"Yes to both. I'd be delighted. What is your address?"

"I'm in Kensington. The address is on this card.."

"Until then."

"Sì, until then."

Angelica had applied on-line to Harvard International Programs, and was delighted to be accepted as an exchange student. It had been his junior year; Daniel's senior.. They had actually met at St. Paul's Church, the nearest one to the campus, on Mt. Auburn St. in Cambridge.

What had drawn the two together was the fact that Daniel detected Mario's accent while seated near him during mass. Daniel's compulsion to learn more of the mysteries of Rome was a magnet. Thereafter, the two planned classes together for the second semester, even double dating at times. Though they exchanged email addresses, their contact gradually diminished as the reality of their individual lives took root.

"Prince Julian, would you please take your rightful place on the throne over the Stone of Destiny?"

"Thank you, Dr. Bilderberger, it will be my pleasure to do so."

As the sparkling crown was placed upon his head, fierce streaks of brilliant lightening flashed through the heavens.

*What the hell is that?* Daniel wondered. There was hardly a cloud in the sky. And just who was that man claiming that he is the rightful ruler? As the lights blinked, heavy raindrops began beating on the roof. *I shall not use his tactics, but I **will** get to my brother and his "queen," so help me, God.*

# Chapter Forty-nine

---

Daniel was a guest at the Duke Hotel. Little could he have imagined that his room was only three doors away from the one which had been occupied by Hemmati when he had taken out Jabaldi a few months previously. Daniel had chosen the fabulous location strictly because of his fascination with the street, which bore his own selected surname. Knowing that it would require considerable manipulative planning to reach his brother, he had returned to the Duke following the coronation via taxi. Pulling out his cell, he punched in Margaret's programmed number. *Much simpler than going through the hotel's system,* he reasoned, *and safer.* The signal was high.

"Hello, Mother."

"Did it really happen? I couldn't bear to watch the television."

"Yes, Mother," Daniel sighed. "We are now members of the world royal family, I presume. I'm still going to find a way to contact them. Get in touch with Klarissa and assure her that I'm up to this."

"Do you have a plan, or is all this just lip service?"

"I didn't get where I am by mere lip service, Mother. Tomorrow I'm on top of it. One of my old classmates from college is here. He works for Julian, as a matter of fact. I'm having dinner with him. Oh, by the way, have you ever heard of an American named Jovan Stewart? Spelled the other way?"

"Oh, like the fake Stuarts?"

"Mother! There are no fake Stuarts! Don't act so daft!'

"I seem to forget that you aren't familiar with my increased corniness that results from intensely nervous circumstances. No. I'm afraid I don't know anyone named Jovan at all...by any surname. Why do you ask?'

"The guy showed his butt at the coronation,  claiming that Julian isn't the true king, he is!"

"Interesting. We'll have to find out what is behind his claim."

"That we will, Mother, that we will. I'll get back to you when I know anything."

After Margaret's call, Klarissa lay on her bed in a fetal position and sobbed.

# Chapter Fifty

The trio of bobbies shoved Jovan harshly into the back of their Armed Response Vehicle.

"You'll all be sorry!" he squawked, wiggling his fingers as if he half expected to work his hands loose.

"Just shut th' bloody 'ell up, Jacko! We're a takin' ya in, we are!"

"Get my cell phone out of my jacket and let me call my lawyer!"

"Nothin' doin', Jack! Ye'll 'av yer chance when ya git ta th' Yard! We're almost there!"

As the ARV pulled in, it was met by a familiar face. The tall man opened the door, and took Jovan by the hand. A smile lit up his rough, lightly-whiskered face.

"Hey, Mike! We hadn't seen ya around fer a spell! Thought ya were still in the states! Didn't ya take a job o're there? Virginia, didn' they say?"

"Hey, Pete, Johnny, see you fellas have a new man with ya?"

"Yeah. This here's Jerry. Ya didn' tell us why yer back."

"Yeah, right. I've been on special assignment in America. I've been like, undercover over there. They hired me in as a Police Chief in Richmond. I was brought back here ta take care of any political prisoners who may come in. They want me ta handle Stewart here. I got a call he was comin' in. I'll book 'im. Ya know why you were brought in, don't you, Stewart? Of course ya do.

"I'll take 'im in and print 'im, boys. Come on, Stewart."

"I didn't do anything to be brought in. I need to call my lawyer!"

"Inside, Stewart, let's go!"

As the three bobbies shut the door in front of them, Mongomery's surly voice grew rigid and raspy. "You're mine, Stewart! Don't think you're gonna make trouble for the new king. We know who you are."

Jovan Stewart's mind flew into high gear. A British cop who had been in America, now had come back from Virginia. Not only that, but the cop knew his identity. He could only have been hired by the powers that be. His only chance was to escape. Alone with Montgomery, he bolted and ran, darting behind the revolving metal sign.

*Just my lucky break*. "Come back or I'll shoot!"

Jovan tore from behind the sign, dashed past a bobbie entering on a motorcycle, and across a lane of traffic on Broadway. The hands cuffed behind his back were an inconvenience, but he had no choice.

Montgomery raised his gun and took aim, the bullet tearing into the back of his target. Dark blood spurted through the fall air as flesh ripped. The late Cardinal Jabaldi's male contact now lay motionless on the ground.

# Chapter Fifty-one

The foliage in Virginia was showing the first tinges of autumn. Nearing the end to the natural photosynthesis cycle, sunlight, coupled with cool nights, was causing the glucose trapped in the maple leaves to create the loveliest of crimson and orange hues. The metamorphosis was breathtaking as Klarissa gazed from her window, aching to escape her loneliness, longing for Julian; not the "King of the World," but merely her husband. Her heart throbbed as her past roamed in and out of her consciousness. The medications that she now appeared to be dependent upon were not aiding her in the need for true love.

With him, again, he was reaching to embrace her. They were on a vacation in Vermont, celebrating their first anniversary. The image in her mind seemed to be all that remained of Julian. Had it truly only been a year? A classic white chapel graced the hillside in front of them; its arrow-like spire piercing the heavens, seeming to point to God.

But where was God now? What symbol could indicate the path heavenward? Was everyone and everything eternally doomed to hellish disaster and emptiness? Would the abyss engulf her in its dark, heckling embrace?

"Klarissa, you have a phone call. You may take it in my office." The kind softness of Lucy Mathers' voice seemed to knock the edge away from her sorrow. Lucy had been a friend indeed, just not all that she needed.

"Thanks, Lucy. I'm right behind you."

Klarissa arose from the bed, her slim form eagerly trailing along. *Good news, it has to be. Anything else I can't take.*

Daniel had arrived back at the Duke, thinking about how he could possibly approach Angelica about his relationship to Julian. But first he must give his other old friend a call. Knowing that he had made London his home, he easily located the number in the phone book.

"Hello. Is my old pal, Gerald around?"

The lady on the line broke into gasping tears.

"Judith? Is that you? This is Daniel St. James. What's wrong?"

"Daniel, I'm sorry I hadn't tried to call you. I know Gerry talked to you not long before…" Her voice cracked, and she was sobbing again.

"Judith, don't tell me something happened to Gerry!"

"Daniel, he told you about the cardinal—Jabaldi…you know what happened to him."

"Yes, but what does that have to do with Gerald?"

"After his death, Gerald inherited everything, you know…"

"The information on the prophecy, the manuscript, and everything?"

"Yes. Well, after Jabaldi's death Gerry got a complex. It was like it took him over…revenge! He went after the assassin, and…"

"Are you telling me that damned assassin killed Gerry?!"

Judith again was in tears, gasping and reaching for her Albuterol.

"I am so sorry, but I hope I'm on to something. Maybe this isn't over yet. You get some rest. I'll get to the bottom of this if it's the last thing I do."

Stepping into the restaurant, Daniel noticed a dark figure seated in the rear. A chill ran down his spine. An amiable waiter came and took his order. He could feel the eyes of the stranger as though they were piercing his soul. As he signed the bill, the stranger brushed past him. He was acutely aware that he was not alone any more.

The entry doors of New Scotland Yard flew open. The bobbies who had turned Stewart over to Montgomery were rapidly followed by others.

"What th' 'ell 'appened, Mike?" Pete cried.

"Stewart tried to escape. Don't know what got into that bloke. I had to shoot 'im. He's down across th' road. We've gotta go get 'im."

"Well, he can't do much. He's cuffed." Jerry said matter-of-factly.

"Bloody well, but I'm takin' no chances," He held his other hand out to signal the traffic to stop.

As the delegation reached the downed prisoner, they saw no motion. The shot had ripped through and into his heart.

Klarissa reached for the phone, her hand trembling.

"Hello?"

"Hello, Klarissa. Daniel called from London..."

"Did they really do it? Is my Julian now king?" Klarissa's voice waivered.

"Listen, Klarissa. I want to tell you the good news..."

"My God, they went through with it!"

"Please, dear, listen. Daniel has an old friend who works for Julian...for the One World Government, somehow. He's meeting with him. He told me to tell you that he will get to the bottom of this. I trust him. He's our hope. Please, I know it's tough, but we must have faith."

"God has forsaken me. My husband is with another woman, and you tell me to have faith?" Klarissa broke into tears.

"Come now, Klarissa, it's time for your meds." Lucy inwardly cringed, knowing that she was hurting so badly.

The line went dead. Margaret said a silent Hail Mary. There was surely a time for all things, and now was the time for faith.

# Chapter Fifty-two

---

Daniel paid the driver before pressing the button at the massive wrought-iron gate. The wheels of thought constantly revolved in his complex brain. *What a break. I must be coy, but persistent.*

"Is that you, mio amico?"

"Yes, of course. You were expecting the king?"

"Oh, but I would have asked the same of him." Angelica's voice resonated as clearly through the intercom as if he were standing there in the flesh.

The huge, well-oiled gates gradually eased open. Daniel felt a smile form on his thin lips. *That's what I'm counting on.*

"What a delicious meal, Megan." Daniel put his left hand on his bulging stomach, and with his right, pushed back from the table.

"My lovely bride is quite skilled in the culinary arts. She is capable of heading a team of chefs at any of the finer eateries in London...or Rome, for that matter."

"Yes, Mario. You married well." Daniel grinned and nodded.

"Gracie! But I did not do so badly, my-self, no?"

Megan Parizo was an ultra-slender, sterling specimen of an Italian woman. Her olive skin was as soft as a baby's. Mario met her while working at the Vatican. Her parents had lived in a platonic relationship for several years after her birth. Her mother's only need for a hus-band was to father a child who would care for her after Mother Nature threw her in the trash bin. So far, her health was holding well. She had been 37 at the time of Megan's birth, and was now 65.

"Could we have some time in private?" Daniel dreaded even asking.

"Megan and I have no secrets."

"Certainly not." Daniel said. *That is doubtful.* "But I have a subject which could be very touchy in her presence."

"My love, do you mind?"

"Of course not." Megan smiled softly. "I have things to attend to in the kitchen. Why don't you old amicos talk in your study?"

"I don't know where to begin, Mario. You know I was reared in an orphanage. I never knew either of my parents."

"Yes, my friend; that I know."

"What would you say if I told you that I have found my birth family?"

"I would say 'Praise God!'"

"There's a lot more. I don't know what you will think…if you will even believe me…"

"Have I ever doubted you, mio amico? You have never given me reason to see you for anything other than who you are—a most honest and trustworthy friend. Of course, just tell me! Someone I met in your country?"

"Not long ago my wife received a phone call from a woman whom I had never met. She said her name was Maggie Dupree. She let Angela know that she had an urgent message for me which was concerning a family matter. Apparently Angela felt like she was a prankster, and hung up on her.

"Later, she paid a visit at our home, uninvited. Angela didn't want to let her in, so I went to the door to see what the problem was. She told us her name was really Margaret Stuart, and she was from Virginia…"

"Not the mother of King Julian who died!"

"Hear me out. The answer is not that simple."

"Either it is yes, or no." Mario's face began to tighten.

"It was indeed the lady you think, but the story gets thicker. She looked so sincere, and my gut just wouldn't let me shut her out.

"She relayed a story to me which had a strange ring of truth to it. She told me that she had given birth to a son who was switched in the hospital. He was born on my birthday. Her husband, Jordon, had instigated the switch..."

"Had anyone else, other than you, said such a thing I would turn him over to the authorities!"

"There's more, much more. Having traced the sealed files, she convinced me that I am truly her son. Sister Rosa at the orphanage had introduced me to a man when I was a young lad who was watching out for my well-being. Margaret showed me a picture of him at my age. There was not the slightest doubt. Jordon Stuart is my father. But here is the clincher...he had an ancient manuscript hidden in a vault which proclaimed that the long-awaited 'messiah' who would rule the world would match the description of Julian, the baby who was substituted for me."

"Jesus, Mary and Joseph! You surely don't believe this?" *He knows about the manuscript. Something is not a fantasy here.* "But Margaret Stuart is dead. How can any of this be checked out?"

"Please, you must swear on your mother's grave that you will not tell a soul what I am about to say."

"I swear, mio amico."

"Margret is alive. I spoke with her just yesterday."

Mario was finding himself in a state of shock. What were the implications here? After an eerie silence, he finally spoke.

"Give me some time, Daniel. I need to think."

"I'm staying at the Duke. Please call me as soon as you are ready. I need a favor. A big favor. I need to see my brother. Oh, and one more thing. The lady with him is not his real wife."

# Chapter Fifty-three

Julian rose to address the newly-formed World Delegation for Arab-Israeli Relations. It was Tuesday, September 18. The conference was being held in the Grand Meeting Room of the plush palace bunker in Jerusalem where he had met with the OWSC while being briefed on his upcoming responsibilities.

This prestigious group included the top personnel from all sectors involved. Very expressly, the leadership of the OIC, the Organization of the Islamic Conference, whose objective for some years had been to promote Islam throughout the world, in order to extol the virtues of a reincarnation of the Caliphate. They envisioned a world run by a "Khilāfah" with both political and civil authority. Julian could never have ascended to his destined throne without a previous agreement with this powerful organization. Extremist groups like the Taliban and al Qaeda, though not bowing to their whims, would thereby acknowledge their alliances. These had agreed to send representatives to the conference.

The PLO, Palestine Liberations Organization, was duly represented. And on the flip side of the Middle-Eastern coin, the Israeli Government, the International Fellowship of Christians and Jews, and British Israelism proponent groups were also represented. Julian was ready. The hot topic would be addressed; the rebuilding of the Temple.

"Ladies and gentlemen of this most austere and noted delegation, once again a zenith has been ascended, a mountain has been scaled. Our awesome campaign is coming to a victorious climax. For the first time since the age of our father, Abraham, we have been able to bring together in one location, under desirable circumstances, the three streams of our heritage and faith. And in so doing, it is my solemn pledge to Israeli and Arab alike that I, as your leader, will consider each of your demands, and the wishes of the Prophet Muhammad, himself; I will judge fairly for all. Our Peace Accord shall not fail..."

A slight murmur arose from the Israeli Prime Minister, but the looks about him quickly brought a dulling silence. Julian continued.

"The OIC has been concerned about their desire for a Caliph. Our committee has worked diligently to make certain that this will happen. Our great religions shall work in harmony. The new Caliph will rule as an Islamic leader, a spiritual and civil judge over the Islamic world. The Bahá'i faith has taught us much about unity and finding common grounds to combat religious prejudice. I wish to express my great thanks to all who have worked so tirelessly on this enterprise. You have accomplished the impossible; bringing together the formerly unyielding groups to instigate a true peace.

"As for our Zionists, considered the most radical of our Israeli delegates, you will not be let down. The Temple, which has been your dream since Herod's second Temple was destroyed by the armies of Titus in 70 CE, is now scheduled to be rebuilt!"

*Now he is singing my song.* The Prime Minister began clapping slowly, then more rapidly, while the applause of his associates joined in the chorus.

Julian continued.

"As some of you are aware, the United Nations, now a part of OWC, has been in control of Jerusalem since 1999. In negotiations between OIC, the PLO, the Israeli government and the International Zionist Movement, and the Knights Templar, a compromise has been reached in which the Dome of the Rock and the Al Aqsa Mosque shall co-exist, side by side with the new Temple. Construction is slated to begin forthwith.

The conference was beaming around the globe. Every eye was upon the new king.

# Chapter Fifty-four

Tuesday was grinding to a close. Daniel had not heard from Angelica. He had called Margaret that morning, telling her of his talk with his friend, using his cell. He would make no more calls from the motel line like the one to Mario. He had felt uneasy since his encounter with the mystical figure in the restaurant. He drew the heavy curtain and gazed out at the pink-streaked sunset.

*Gerald told me that Jabaldi was on a quest to locate the manuscript. That may be the key!*

He sat down in the recliner, pushed the lever and allowed his legs to be raised to waist level. As he reached for the TV remote, the room phone buzzed.

"Mio amico!"

"Hey, amico, let me call you back!"

Daniel quickly retrieved his cell from his pocket and dialed the number.

"Mario, sorry about this, but I think I may have a bug somewhere. Hell, the whole damn hotel may be bugged. I haven't found anything on my phone. Anyway, after I got back here following the Coronation I called Mother. I already told you about that, but later, I tried to call my old pal, Gerry Houseman. His fiancé told me that he had been killed while trying to avenge Jabaldi's murder. That evening when I went downstairs for dinner, I was being watched by an eerie Middle-Eastern-looking man. Gerry told me that the cardinal had been searching for the manuscript. The one I told you about with the Gnostic prophecy. I can't help but feel that this is all tied together somehow.

Angelica cleared his throat.

"Mio amico, I have decided to help you. Meet me at the foot of the tower tomorrow at noon.

"The tower?"

"Big Ben."

# Chapter Fifty-five

As the monstrous clock chimed for the twelfth time, Daniel St. James slowly turned his head in every imaginable position trying to figure out why Angelica had not yet arrived.

*He set the time and place, for heaven sake!*

The clock ticked on. Five more minutes, then ten. A pigeon dropping fell, narrowly missing Daniel's head. His thoughts began darting to the frightening possibilities. *What if Gerry's assassin has found him? If he had bugged our call the first time, could the trace have been on Mario's end?*

"Mio amico, sorry I'm a bit late."

Daniel blew out a relieved sigh.

"Sorry if I was a bit paranoid, Mario, but I think I'm being watched."

"Understandable, amico. We're dealing with a force bigger than even you could possibly imagine. I wanted to meet out here so I could be assured that no one could hear us. The outdoor air will do neither of us harm.

Daniel smiled. "What do you have for me?"

"Well, I knew about the manuscript. It is housed in a safe, in Jerusalem, at the World Bank, in a plush bunker. Only five persons have access to it."

"And would you know who those five privileged individuals might be?"

"Certainly, mio amico. Prince Julian, your father, General Lorraine, Dr. Bilderberger, and..."

"And?"

"And myself."

# Chapter Fifty-six

"**W**ow! The next question would be the logical one. Are you willing to risk your future for an old friend...and most importantly, for the truth?"

"If I were not willing to help you I would not have come. Remember the old adage; *the truth will set you free*?

Daniel St. James nodded and smiled. "Of course, my friend, of course. In truth, that saying is more than an old adage. It comes from the Gospel of John, chapter eight, verse thirty-two. I had to memorize it in parochial school. They are the very words of Jesus as spoken to the Jewish believers. So what is next?"

"We must leave at once for Israel, but on separate flights."

Daniel's flight arrived at noon the following day, Thursday. He knew that his friend was already there. Angelica had asked for three days leave of duties to spend time researching in Israel. Since his loyalty was unquestioned, and his top aide was prepared to handle any impending emergency, his request was quickly granted. At least there was no need to hide the fact that he was taking a flight to Jerusalem.

All Daniel could do now was wait. His instructions had been explicit. He must remain in the park in West Jerusalem until Mario arrived. He looked at his Rolex. The meeting was to occur at precisely 2:40. While that gave him a mere 15 minutes, in this context, it would seem like an eternity.

Deep in the heart of the bunker, ten floors beneath the lobby of the colossal bank, his friend had been granted admission by right thumb scan and the spoken password. Cautiously, he reached into the drawer and lifted the priceless treasure, placing it securely into a molded tube, before fastening the latch. As he quickly exited, forcing the massive vault door back into place, he heard voices along with the quickening pattering of feet.

# Chapter Fifty-seven

$A$ world away, Klarissa was just awaking. It was 8:35 A.M. Eastern Standard Daylight Savings time in Virginia. Nervously she rubbed her eyes. A premonition flashed across the screen of her mind. Something was happening; she could feel it with all certainty. *Where do these sensations come from?*

Suddenly, the phone rang at the desk.

"Klarissa, dear, it's for you. Your mother-in-law."

Mario Angelica walked nonchalantly down the hall toward the elevator. The approaching guards were at his side.

"Greetings, gentlemen, what can I do for you today?" Angelica smiled and reached out his hand, his pyramid insignia clearly in view. *Thank God I wore my uniform.*

"Good afternoon, sir. We were returning from break and heard the doors close to the vault. We were not expecting you." The guard's expression turned from a picture of panic to one of relative ease.

"It's good to know that we have such dedicated personnel guarding our most valued assets. Mario Angelica," he said, extending for the handshake, "Special Vatican Envoy."

"Pleased to meet you, Captain. Ansell Jacobi, sir, and this is my partner on the afternoon shift, James Pearlman." Pearlman nodded and Jacobi continued, "I've heard all the talk about you. Of course, I also knew that you were on the short list of those who are permitted in the vault."

"I am in your great city doing some research for the Vatican, and came by to check on some files. Carry on, gentlemen. Have a pleasant day."

Angelica stepped into the elevator and pushed the button. The two guards looked at each other and frowned.

"Something doesn't seem kosher," Jacobi said. "Angelica's visit was not announced. I'm calling Bilderberger."

As Mario emerged from the World Bank, a slight, dry breeze was blowing. It was sunny and 28 degrees Celsius; just the weather he enjoyed most. He waved down the first taxi and headed for the center of the Old City. He paid the driver and stepped out onto Hillel Street.

The trees had barely begun to turn in Gan Ha'Atzmout, also called Independence Park. As he reached the rock-lined walkway into the park, he accelerated his gate. Daniel's face lit up, as he jolted from the grass where he had been sitting, reaching out to embrace him.

"Thank God. Let's get out of here," he said.

"This better be good, Jacobi, I'm in the sauna."

"Yes, Your Highness, I'm concerned. Mario Angelica entered the vault today unannounced."

"The vault?" Bilderberger froze for a few crystal seconds, then continued, "He has clearance, but only when authorized. Do you have someone on his tail?"

"No, Your Highness. I wanted to talk with you about this first. I thought there was a possibility that he was here on official business for the king or yourself.

Jacobi was one of a handful of persons who knew Bilderberger for who he truly was — the undisputed CEO of world royalty — the supreme authority behind the powers that be.

"Hello, Klarissa. Are you feeling well? Are they treating you like the princess you are *supposed* to be?"

"Oh, Margaret!" Klarissa didn't know whether to smile or cry. "You shouldn't be humoring me. Have you any news from our Daniel?"

"Today he is in Jerusalem. I can't say more until this is wrapped up, dear. But I pray, if I dare do such sacrilege with the doubts which have enveloped me, that God is real and working on our behalf."

Klarissa felt a rapid ripple of chills run down her spine. *Jerusalem!* The horrid memories of her daunting entrapment seemed to drown her soul in gloominess.

"Klarissa? Are you there?"

"Yes, I'm here. Better here than there!"

"I'm sorry, dear. I can't even begin to imagine what you and Becky went through…"

"No, you can't. Please, just keep me informed. And can you also call Gloria?"

"She's near the top of my call list."

"Can't you even give me a hint as to what is happening there?"

"Daniel thought it better merely to tell you that he has a powerful connection, and that he hopes to be able to get to Julian soon. We must think positive thoughts, mustn't we?"

"I have faith in Daniel, Maggie, and somehow, I'm learning to believe in God."

Margaret's smile came through the phone as surely as if by Skype. "Goodbye, dear. I'll call you at first word of contact with your husband."

Klarissa handed the cordless handset to Lucy and headed for the kitchen and her morning coffee.

# Chapter Fifty-eight

---

Chills swept over Daniel's skin as the two passed the Lions Cave, where legend has it that a pious lion guarded the remains of the early Christian Martyrs. Both men were aware of the rich history of the park including the grave in the ancient Muslim Mamilla Cemetery on the east end containing the domed grave of the Mamluk Emir Aidughi Kubaki, thirteenth-century governor of Allepo and Safed, who was exiled to Jerusalem before his death in 1289. While he had been seated in the grass beneath the forked tree, he had only allowed brief thoughts of the history to run past him. The mission at hand was what was possessing him; now it was time for the unadulterated truth.

Mario had made a discrete appointment with his friend at the Israel Antiquities Authority in the Rockefeller Museum Building. In the cab on the way, the driver was sure they were en route to a funeral.

"Dr. Ben-Dura! Mario Angelica!" His voice personified anticipation.

Around the world, David Ben-Dura was considered as the leading expert in the authenticity of antiques. He was particularly noted for his work in reference to ancient scrolls, inks and fabrics. Hired by the Antiquities Authority in 2002, he had examined everything from the Dead Sea Scrolls to a fragment of the Shroud of Turin, the latter as a special favor to Mario Angelica. There was not a shred of doubt in the Envoy's mind that this doctor's findings would be based on scientific proof, and never on any personal agenda.

"I am eager to see this supposed relic. I have heard the legends and claims of our new 'king,' and now I am privileged to be able to see for myself."

Gingerly Mario removed the manuscript from the tube before handing it to the doctor. St. James' mouth dropped as the scroll was unrolled upon the counter. *My God! It is unbelievable!*

Klarissa sat pensively at the plain wooden table, thankfully sipping her coffee. *Please, God, if you are there, unravel this tangled web and bring my husband home to me.*

In New Orleans, Gloria was walking the floor.

# Chapter Fifty-nine

Inside the courtyard of the Rockefeller Museum stands one of the most ancient pine trees in all of Israel. According to Arab legend, it was here that Ezra the scribe wrote the Torah for Israel. The Antiquities Authority was most pleased, indeed, to have this third location for their offices since its founding in 1948.

The powerful lights automatically lowered closer to the ancient document before Ben-Dura positioned a powerful microscope near the upper edge of the cloth, which he had placed closest to him. He then began the sensitive unrolling process, wearing soft, lamb-skin gloves.

Mario had related both the supposed history of the manuscript and the dangers involved in obtaining and keeping it.

"Uh-huh, uh-huh…"

"Uh-huh, what?" St. James said with a touch of quivering in his voice.

"This manuscript is very ancient. It appears to be at least two thousand years old, at first observation. It is papyrus, such as that used in scripting the Dead Sea Scrolls, the fragments of the Torah and the Ryland Library Papyrus, all of which I have examined, but it appears older than the latter.

"There is no doubt that the material is authentic. The papyrus reed is a bulrush, exactly like that in which the Tanakh tells us Moses was hidden as an infant. It is usually thought of as growing on the banks of the Nile in Egypt. However, this type of reed was also grown in a small district of Sicily. I'm going to need to run some extensive tests on both the fabric and the ink. If this is a fake, it is one of the finest I have ever seen. We must be certain. May I keep the manuscript?"

Angelica and St. James looked at one another, but both spoke at once. "Yes, we *must* know."

"But you understand, this is a matter of extreme security," Mario continued. "Any or all of us could be in dire danger from the powers that be. This cannot be emphasized enough."

"Understood, my friend."

Meanwhile, Bilderberger answered his phone again. "Yes? What this time?"

"It's the manuscript, Your Highness. It's missing!"

"I'll take care of this traitor. He's dead meat!"


Bilderberger immediately called Vatican security to ask about Mario. To his feigned surprise, he was told that he was in Israel on personal business.

"Personal business, eh? Might you know the nature of the business?"

"He is meeting with an old friend to discuss investments."

"Investments, hell," he mumbled as he shut off his smart phone.

The next call was to Megan Angelica.

"Hello, young lady. This is Dr. Bilderberger. Is your husband about?"

Megan paused. *Why would he be calling Mario? He never has called here before?*

"Hello, doctor. No, my husband is in Israel on business. Can I have him call you when he returns? He should be home tomorrow."

"No, ma'am. Do you have a number where I can reach him? I tried his cell number that we have on file and got no answer."

"Strange thing, he called me from the airport to tell me he had forgotten his cell and that he would be back in touch tonight. Could I tell him you called?"

"That won't be necessary. I'll get back to him later. Have a great day, Mrs. Angelica." *That's one hell of a note. I'll deal with him. That bastard has no place to hide.*

# Chapter Sixty

The brilliant Israeli sun was barely beginning to rise as Mario arrived via taxi at Alarot Airport.

"There he is," a distinctive voice spoke into a BlackBerry. "I'll have him soon."

Daniel had purposely used Ben Gurion International in Tel Aviv, 45 kilometers southwest of Jerusalem. His return ticket was purchased for the Big Apple. Meeting his brother was going to have to wait.

"That's my man. I knew I could count on you. I want him taken alive," the harsh voice snapped into the phone. "This is *not* a hit. Take him to the bunker and I will meet you there tonight at twenty hundred hours."

Angelica shook himself. What had happened? Where was he? Suddenly he found himself glaring up into the face of Joshua Bilderberger.

"Okay, wise guy. Where is it?"

Mario's eyes widened as they attempted to focus. Surely not — he couldn't be back in the bunker!

"Where is *what*? How did I get here?"

"You know freaking well what I'm after. Now what did you do with it, and who is in this with you?" The back of his right hand met hard with his captive's right jaw, his massive diamond ring tearing into the flesh, causing a gush of dark blood and a resounding scream.

"Mario Antonio Angelica, number 745369, Vatican Special Envoy!"

"You bloody idiot, answer me."

"Mario Antonio Angelica, num…" A second strike, this time Bilderberger's fist, connected with Angelica's left jaw, and the sound of cracking bone echoed through the chamber.

"Just who the bloody hell do you think you're fooling with here, clown?!"

"I am well aware of your identity, Dr. Bilderberger."

"You are either an imbecile or you have no idea of my *position* in the scheme of things! Now tell me what I want to know or I'll…"

"You'll what, kill me? Then how will you find your priceless manuscript?" Mario forced a fake smile through bloodshot eyes.

"Listen, you bastard, I'm giving you ten minutes to come up with the truth, or you will wish you'd never been born!"

Angelica said a silent "Hail Mary" just before he floated away into unconsciousness.

In an adjoining room, Hemmati sipped a Raki. He had learned to appreciate their value while on a mission in Turkey. This one was a suma mixed with ethanol in copper alembics which he had bought on the black market in the Arab Section of Jerusalem. He laughed and shook his head ever so slightly. *Most people have no idea what they could get if they only knew where to look.*

Hemmati had made contact with the One World Scientific Committee shortly following his hit on Gerald Houseman. After relating to the contact person the nature of his business, along with the fact that it had been he who has erased Cardinal Jabaldi, getting to Bilderberger had not been so difficult. He had made certain that his agreement was quid pro quo. After all, someone of his specially-honed skills would be of more value working for the OWSC than against them.

# Chapter Sixty-one

---

Dr. Ben-Dura had known better than to leave the mysterious manuscript lying about the museum, or even in his office in the Antiquities Authority. Hopefully no one would suspect that it was in his possession, but it was for certain that he could take no unnecessary chances.

The day of their visit, he had reinserted it into the special tubular container, thereafter placing it in his Escalade for transport to his home in nearby Bethlehem. Who would suspect tiny Bethlehem? It would be like saying that a king would be born there, right?

A widower, he lived alone in a modest two-story box-style house, with a palm tree and a tiny patch of grass. On the street floor, in the rear, he also had an additional gigantic building that housed a laboratory, one that was enclosed in a gated yard where he would go to be alone in order to better study the great scrolls of historic significance; those that might sometimes fall into his hands by virtue of friends like Mario.

With no personal indebtedness, he had spared no expense in equipping this haven of his with the finest of energy-saving florescent lighting, microscopes, containers, testing supplies and previously-prepared chemical solutions. There were also numerous refrigeration units, a modern dating machine and a computer system beyond its time.

The fact that Israel ranks first in the world in personal computers per capita had made it unproblematic for him to shop the market for the best and most capable software. He was able to snap 400 dpi photos so as to view their remarkable images in gigantic magnification on his 155mm LCD monitor hanging from the wall.

A team of chemists had made sure that no need which might arise would ever go unfulfilled. A top-notch chemist, himself, Ben-Dura kept them on their toes. He was able to analyze materials such as the papyrus of the manuscript and the inks used therein, dating them with absolute accuracy.

His skills had been sharpened by years of study, not only at Hamline University, but also on his own time. A leading expert in linguistic peculiarities, such additional insight allowed him to easily resolve enigmas such as by whom and when a text had been written.

Since no major current events of the era in which it was written were mentioned in this "prophetic scroll," that consideration had gone out the window. In this instance, his knowledge of Paleography, the study of ancient handwriting, would also be a major advantage. Because he had no clue as to the true history of their discovery, the claim that they were unearthed by the original Templars from under the Temple mount in Jerusalem was also a major concern in his evaluation.

That night he had mounted the edge of the ancient papyrus cautiously in a dual clamp. Rolling it out about one arm's length, he took close-up photos of the text. It was obviously ancient Hebrew, not Aramaic, but in comparisons with that of other writings from the Midrash, particularly Kabalistic, how did this rate? The photo snapping was followed up by a minor scraping of ink which was thicker than that found in most places. The ink had to be tested for both origin and composition.

Ben-Dura was so filled with excitement at the examination of this mystic manuscript that he could hardly dream of sleeping.

The approximate age seemed evident, but the carbon-14 dating would close the gap. In this most accurate of tests of its type, the age of a document is based on the rate of decay of the radioactive or unstable carbon isotope 14, known as 14C. Electron emission to Nitrogen 14 is then measured, which determines the "half life" of the material or substance being tested.

Clipping a small strip from the border, he began the test. He then placed it in the chemicals for pre-preparation, which would take two days. He immediately downloaded the snapshots to his computer so that he was able to begin viewing the results on the giant monitor. Yes, there was a slightly different texture to this papyrus...

The first test on the initial ink sample was inconclusive, so he ran it again. Uh-huh!

Exhausted, the doctor flopped into bed at 2:45 A.M.

The night brought no results from Angelica. Out of sheer exasperation, Bilderberger bound his prisoner and retired.

"Your turn, Bilderberger snapped impatiently to Hemmati as he motioned toward the holding room the next morning. Just make damn sure you don't kill him; at least not until he comes clean with us."

The assassin smiled wickedly, nudging his way between the guards into the darkened chamber.

"Hello? Mrs. Angelica?" It was later than usual when the doctor arose on Friday, but he had a museum to manage and an agency to run. He had called the cell on which he had reached his friend in the past.

"Yes. Who is calling, please?"

"This is a friend of your husband in Israel. I am just a bit surprised that you are answering his cell phone. Is Mario available?"

"I was going to ask you the same thing. He was supposed to fly in this morning, but he never showed up. Did you see him yesterday?"

"Yes. He informed me that he would be returning there, just as you indicated." Ben-Dura dropped and shook his head. "This is not a good thing. Is my number showing up on that phone?"

"Yes."

"Then write it down, memorize it and erase it. Call me if you hear anything. I'm afraid your husband is in over his head. No fault of his own, ma'am."

"Can you please tell me what is going on?"

"Telling you that would not be good for your wellbeing, ma'am. But whatever you do, do not give out this number. Not only my life, but the future of the world could be in danger."

# Chapter Sixty-two

---

As soon as Megan Angelica laid the BlackBerry on the table, she could feel the tears trickle down her smooth olive cheeks. There was only one thing to do. She must contact Daniel St. James. Her mind was whirling. If this involved the OWSC, then calling from the cell would not be wise. In fact, she would go to a pay phone at a nearby hostel. She would take euro coins — these obviously could not be detected. *It's a wonder I can even think! But thank God, I can!*

"St. James residence, may I help you?" Daniel wiped his eyes. He had gone to bed early because he still had jet lag.

"Daniel, this is Megan Angelica. I'm afraid something awful has happened. Mario didn't come home yet. Both Bilderberger and someone from Israel called asking for him! I was told that he may be in grave danger!"

"My God!" St. James gasped. "I will do my best to locate him. Time may be of the essence right now. I'll get back to you...or maybe you had better call me. I have a throw-away cell for emergencies. The number is 804-555-6392. Give me 15 hours."

Daniel got dressed and pulled the disposable phone from the drawer by his bed.

"Hello, Israel Antiquities Authority."

"Dr. Ben-Dura! Thank God you're okay. Are you the one who called Mario's wife a while ago?"

"Yes, I am. Is this line secure? Can it be traced?"

"Yes and no. It's untraceable. Apparently you haven't heard from our mutual friend."

"No, and I'm very concerned! He was not on the flight back to Rome. I called the airport since I first talked with Mrs. Angelica. I fear he's in the hands of the OWSC here in Jerusalem, and at the top level."

"I have a schematic of the bank building where their headquarters is. This is also where Angelica retrieved the relic. Is there anyone we can trust to investigate until I can return and meet you?"

"We'll have to be cautious in meeting. No one can find out at this point that I am involved. I'm too close to having an answer on the origin of the papyrus."

"Yes, with Mario in danger, I hadn't even asked. How's that progressing?"

"I'll save my report until after the carbon-14 dating is complete, but I have already discovered a very unusual feature to this document. I want you to see it in person. You will be as shocked as I was, I'm sure."

Daniel's brow wrinkled. "You certainly have my curiosity peaked. I'm anxious to hear more. When will your findings be complete?"

"Tomorrow night about 9:30."

"And what about someone to contact who would be capable of getting into the bunker?"

Ben-Dura smiled. "Yes, it pays to have friends—of all types. Call 2 033 055 3438856. The man's name is Akim Manassas. Tell him Dr. David sent you. Tell him I said 'El Shaddai.'"

"El Shaddai? That's a name for God. Why would I tell him that?"

The smile was still on Ben-Dura's face. "Yes, it means 'Lord all sufficient.' It's a long story and I won't bore you with it. But it has to do with an incident from our past. If you tell him that, he will know you are genuine and that I really asked you to call him."

That was enough. "Thanks, my friend. I'll need to tell him what's going on."

"Anything you say to him will go to his grave."

"I'll call you later for a mutual update."

# Chapter Sixty-three

---

Hemmati took his empty glass to the restroom and filled it with water, then sauntered into the chamber where Angelica lay motionless on the divan, thrusting it into his blood-splattered face.

"Hey! You filthy piece of crap! Wake up!"

Angelica moaned slightly, his swollen eyes attempting to open. Grasping his shirt collar in his massive left hand, and forcing him to meet his mocking menace, he then used his right hand to squeeze Angelica's chin, jerking his head upward.

"Okay, butthead! I'm going to be nice one time, and give you a chance to redeem your useless self. Then I'm going to make what Bilderberger did to you seem like child's play. *Where* is the manuscript?"

"Why don't you just..."Angelica softly mumbled. His body was racked with pain from the beatings that Bilderberger had inflicted during the night.

"What's that, fruitcake? Did you say something? Speak up. I'm a little hard of hearing.

"Why don't you just finish the job, you coward!" Somehow the words came more loudly, piercing his captor's heart.

The killer instinct within Hemmati ran through him like a bolt of lightning. He pulled a pistol from his belt and aimed it, but just as he was pulling the trigger, Bilderberger jumped through the door and averted the shot.

"That's just what he wanted you to do! Can I *trust* you or not? Right now I'm questioning my decision to hire an assassin to handle a torture assignment!"

The blood was now beginning to return to Hemmati's whitened face. He had lost it. How dare he allow a low-life holy Joe like Angelica to ruin his day!

St. James lost no time contacting Manassas, to whom he freely divulged the details of the complex dilemma which had entangled the lives of his family members, and now seemed to have driven one of his dearest comrades to the brink of oblivion. Following the conversation, he drove to a nearby Kinko's where he could fax the schematics of the World Bank

Building, including its secret bunker, to Manassas at an undisclosed location in Jerusalem.

Calling his office to file a report that he had a family emergency out of state, he then headed for the airport. On the way he phoned his mother with an update as well as a message for Klarissa. "Please don't alarm her, Mother. Tell her that we will have some news within the next couple of days."

"You got it, son. Be careful!"

"Of course, Mother. Don't worry about me. I've got nothing to connect this to me. Mario is a saint, if there ever was one. He'd die before he'd put me in jeopardy. If he makes it out of this I owe him big."

"I'll handle Angelica my frikin' self, Hemmati!"

Bilderberger ordered his goon from the room, and calling in the guards to carry the prisoner to the torture chamber — a room reserved for such extreme cases as this.

So weak and bruised that he was barely conscious, Angelica was lifted by two robust young guards. He was placed in a doubled over position, his head near his knees, and his hands laying on them, before being secured inside a metal circle that dangled from a huge beam near the ceiling. The circular devise was then tightened upon his body by the turning of a crank above his head. As the repulsive machine gradually began crushing its prey Angelica let out screams which resembled a cougar warning her cubs of approaching danger.

"Last chance, traitor! Tell us where you took the manuscript!"

"N-n-never!!!" The screech from his lips was soon accompanied with gushes of blood.

"Release him. We'll give him a few hours to come to his senses." Bilderberger shook his head and slowly walked out of the room.

# Chapter Sixty-four

---

Akim Manassas was a regular at the World Bank, so his entrance that afternoon was totally commonplace. This time, however, he had done some preparation.

Two close associates had disabled the security cameras via a little-known new computer program designed for secret service personnel and hijacked from Mossad by a mole within Metsada, a clandestine operations command, who Manassas paid extremely well. In fact, Metsada turned their heads to his actions, because many times they were very much in conjunction with their own precedence. If need be, Manassas had connections inside both MI6 and the CIA.

In addition, Mario Angelica, the genius that he was, had planned far ahead of this possibility. He had produced a lifelike replica of his right thumb from a mold, complete with seriously realistic vinyl skin, proven to be quite sufficient to fool the entrance requirements, leaving it and his password with the good doctor. This was accomplished with no knowledge of his partner in crime. After the call from St. James, Ben-Dura had sent them via currier to Manassas with a note as to their significance.

Manassas nodded and smiled as he headed for the side door. His partners had each entered unnoticed and were standing in the hall which led to a secure entrance to the passageway which gave access to the secret elevator.

After the cameras had been disabled, a video lasting a full hour had been downloaded onto a DVR which would run and rerun for the next two hours, allowing the team ample time to accomplish their sovereign mission.

Discretely and silently, the door was opened and the Mission-Impossible-style team was on its way to the plush bunker.

On the divan in the holding chamber was sprawled the comatose form of Mario Angeli-ca. In his mind he saw a vision of a bright light which he was approaching. A voice was calling ever so gently. "Son, it's your mother. I'm wait-ing for you..."

In his palace on a hill in Rome, Julian had been alerted to a possible threat and was looking

over an alternative agenda — what to do in case
of subversion.

# Chapter Sixty-five

St. James' plane landed on time. It had taken 13 hours and 26 minutes, including a flight change in New York. Albeit dog-tired, in comparison to Angelica, he was certain that his condition was as fresh as a daisy in May. He had drifted off many times during the long flight across the Atlantic.

He knew from a text he had just received from Ben-Dura that the mission had been a resounding success. The team had noiselessly entered the bunker and rescued his friend without any detection during the time that he was awaiting final interrogation.

Bilderberger was beside himself. He had issued a global APB for Angelica, whom he described as a fearless traitor to all that had made the world a safe place in which to live.

Daniel's first call of thanks was to the doctor. He was assured that his friend had been whisked away in a helicopter which had transported him to a secure location maintained by Manassas, which could administer much-needed medical attention. St. James then received a call from Megan, who assured him that her husband had been rescued from the jaws of death.

For the security of all, there were factors that were working against the OWC, and they did not understand how.

That night Daniel checked into a remote motel near Bethlehem and slept like a baby, with the added assurance that tomorrow would dawn as a new day, one with renewed anticipation of the results which would be final that same night.

"In case of subversion by a large segment or particular group of citizens of the One World, we must not fail to take proper charge. The subversives must be taken into captivity and eradicated. Large cremation vaults have been prepared to handle such a situation.

"A simple explanation will be offered; an alien invasion will be blamed. Our gullible constituents will largely believe that the missing persons were abducted and carried away. In the case of a large number of conservative Christians being involved, some would even believe that the so-called 'rapture' had occurred."

Even in his hypnotic state, Julian seemed dazed.

He laid the document on the desk. "Why was I not included in this decision?"

"My son," Jordan spoke in a soft voice, "These policies had to be put in place before the new government could come forth. As you know, you could only be informed when your time came."

"Let's hope it doesn't come to this, Father."

"You are the man of the hour," Joshua Bilderberger grunted to Hemmati. "This time I don't give a damn. I want Mario Angelica brought back, dead or alive!"

"You're finally speaking in a tongue I can understand."

"Tonight, Mother, I will have more news for you. At least my friend has been spared. Where he is, he will not be found. Even Bin Laden couldn't get to him there."

"That's wonderful, son. I'll tell Klarissa and Gloria that we are getting close."

# Chapter Sixty-six

---

Angelica grunted as his weakened eyes detected the first rays of Saturday sunlight filtering through the brocade white drapes by his bed. The only place he had ever seen that could compare to the conditions around him were those of the sterile bunker in which he had been held captive. He had been in scores of hospitals which seemed clean enough, but this intensive care unit—that had to be what it was—was many cuts above. Whoever had taken him here didn't want him to die, at least.

His pupils began to focus, in and out. Gradually the image of a tender smiling feminine face with heavenly deep-brown eyes, and strands of black, silky hair came into view. She was dressed in pure pallid garments. He felt a tiny smile broaden on his puffy cheeks. Now he knew his impressions of the afterlife were real. He had died and gone to the seventh heaven.

"Good morning, Mr. Angelica. You had quite a rough night. Can you hear me?"

"Did I miss St. Peter on the way in? This is heaven, right?"

The nurse giggled. "Compared to the place from which they tell me you were picked up, I guess you could say this is heaven. But in reality, you are in a hospital at a location which I am not at liberty to tell even you, sir."

Angelica tried to lift his head, and the throbbing in his cranial area and torso was so excruciating that he promptly plopped to the pillow.

"Now I know I'm still on earth! Can you please bring me something for this pain?"

"You've been living on morphine, and I'm only authorized to administer it one more time. After that, we'll have to try other drugs. I assure you, you will get better, it just takes time."

"Thanks. Who brought me here?"

"That's something you'll know in time. Just get some rest. You are to be treated like a king."

St. James stretched his arms upward as his feet hit the carpeted floor. Time had lost all meaning with his continued darting to and fro around the orb. In his mind he knew it was Saturday morning, September 22nd. He was still so stressed by his bizarre adventures that he knew he must be a character in a Stephen King movie. Looking at the digital clock on the nightstand, it said it was 10:47. He had purposely not set an alarm. He needed the rest.

After a shower, and even before eating, his first priority was to call Ben-Dura. Calling from a local phone would never be questioned. Besides, neither of them were under suspicion, to his knowledge.

"Good morning, my friend! Did you rest well?"

"Yes, thank you. I'm getting my bearings. Have there been any indications that you are being watched?"

"None whatsoever. I want you to meet me for dinner; then we will be able to get the final results of the dating. I'll go by my home and take the sample from the solution before we meet. We can then go back to my place in order to go over it together, because then it will be complete."

"Sounds wonderful. Where shall we meet?"

"Divano Café and Restaurant in Bethlehem on Jerusalem Hebron Road. You'll love the food—my treat. Meet me there at 7:30."

"Great. That will give me plenty of time to get my calls done. The restaurant is not far from where I'm staying."

That night at dinner, the doctor refused to make any comment on the manuscript until they had gone to his home for the carbon-14 results.

# Chapter Sixty-seven

---

"Just as I suspected; the carbon-14 dating confirms that this papyrus is indeed over 2000 years old, and the primary ink is one that was also used during that same time frame."

Daniel stared at Ben-Dura and squinted. "Then we're up the creek without a paddle."

"Hear me out. When I initially scraped ink from the papyrus to test for origin, I scraped it from the year, because it was heavier, standing out a little more from the scroll that the previous text. A great amount of this document was undoubtedly penned during the era of the Dead Sea Scrolls, prior to the birth of Jesus. However," Ben-Dura paused, placing sections of the etching on the screen before them, "take a look at this. The translation of the first line of this Hebrew text is:

*"'Early in the year of 5773, in the month of Nisan,'*

"The part of this before the year is original. However, the date has been changed, and the year inserted with a mixture containing both the original ink and iron gall, a common concoction used in the Middle Ages. It is likely that a previous date was replaced by the year 5773. Further down, the same pattern occurs.

*"'a great leader shall discover his destiny.'*

"'Shall discover,' as you see, denoted by the symbols נגלה, also have been altered. Likely it was originally גילה, or 'discovered.' There was very little to do to make this change. Only a small scrape was required.

*"'He shall be called the true messiah, and shall deliver the people from great perils.'*

"'Shall be called,' יקרא, also has been altered slightly. 'Was called' in Hebrew is נקרא, therefore, again, a minor change of one Hebrew symbol was needed, making detection near impossible... and on it goes. Many small alterations were made with this same concoction. In this case, only a small swatch of additional ink was needed.

"It is my expert opinion that this scroll was a historic document regarding a messiah figure, before Jesus.

"Our history records 10 such men, any of which could have been described in this document."

Daniel St. James sighed deeply. "What do you suggest we do now?"

"Under the circumstances there is only one thing to do."

# Chapter Sixty-eight

Mario Angelica had gradually improved, and by Sunday morning, the very next morning, he was able to ask for a priest to serve him mass. Manassas was there to greet him, and only too happy to grant his wish. Because he was on good terms with both Christians and Jews, he called the Church of the Holy Sepulcher, one of a handful of Roman Churches in the area, and sent a limo out to collect, blindfolded, a priest for the Envoy's personal service. In exchange, a hearty donation was made to the church.

Manassas, himself a former member of Masada, was both a friend of peace, and a Zionist of the highest level. The sellout of Rabbi Ginsberg had been a stench in his nostrils. Although he knew that Angelica had been on the OWSC payroll, he also knew where it had gotten him. His future was to take a new route, as after this, so, too, would the world.

As the priest was leaving, two new visitors were entering his room.

"Hello, my old amico!"

Angelica looked up into the beaming faces of Daniel St. James and Dr. Ben-Dura. Never had anyone been so happy to see someone, he thought.

"You look a little worn and torn, my friend," Daniel continued.

"Nothing a month on the French Riviera with my Megan wouldn't cure. I haven't been able to speak to her yet. Do you suppose…"

Just then the curtain opened, and in walked Megan. Angelica's heart beat wildly as he flung open his arms to let her in.

# Chapter Sixty-nine

---

Hemmati had called in every marker he had owing to him. It seemed that Angelica had disappeared into thin air. On Saturday night, Bilderberger had threatened to have his head if he did not produce the traitor *and* the manuscript within 24 hours.

Margaret had phoned both Klarissa and Gloria, telling them that the mystic prophetic manuscript had been proven to be a medieval forgery and that within days they would all be united.

Daniel knew that somehow his brother had to be rescued from his hypnotic trance so that he could be brought back to the real world. Now his hopes lay with Ben-Dura, Manassas and their cronies. But how would these two men be able to accomplish such a feat? While Ben-Dura had definitely meant something by his cryptic remark of "only one thing to do," they were not fighting City Hall; instead, they were literally up against the World.

For now, Daniel had accepted the invitation of Ben-Dura to stay at his home while he and Manassas made their play. Aside from majority ownership of a television network in Israel, which was one definite bonus, and the ability to tap into the World Network, taking over their programming, which was something altogether out of his realm, he was unable to imagine what other connections that this former agent might have had.

Rising on Sunday morning, Margaret clicked the remote to her television. Klarissa was already up and watching CBS Sunday Morning. In Jerusalem, it was 3:00 PM. A sudden shrill tone came forth from every television set, worldwide, that was turned on at that precise moment.

"This is a special worldwide bulletin. The government previously set up by the One World Union came into power under false pretenses. The mysterious 'manuscript' which was said to have prophesied Julian Stuart as the messianic 'Savior of Mankind,' leading to his crowning as king, has been proven beyond a shadow of a doubt to have been a medieval forgery.

"As you are now viewing your television screen, you are witness to that very papyrus. Certain portions, vital to the supposed prophecies, have been altered. The document has been deemed, by a foremost expert in the field of authentication of ancient scrolls, to be nothing more than an ancient historical record inscribed by a rabbi during the 400-year Midrash period of Jewish history between the ending of the writing of the Tanakh, also known as the 'Old Testament,' and the birth of Jesus.

"A conference has just been held involving world leaders, those previously at the helms of governments, who have been serving under the new regime. An immediate proclamation was made calling for both the prompt ouster of the king and the dissolving of the One World Government.

"We now take you live to an undisclosed location in the United States where an announcer is standing by."

"Ladies and gentlemen, I am here with a young lady who is the legal wife of the man we know as King Julian. She and her mother were recently taken by force to Jerusalem and held against their will by Muslim extremists at the demand of the OWSC. Aided by members of the Israeli Government, they were able to escape. After being flown back to America, she was immediately taken into protective custody, waiting in due course for an opportunity to tell her story.

"In danger for her life from the One World Government, she now has the tangible proof with which to relate her story, thanks to an unidentified public servant who will be revealed once this situation is under control and the perpetrators of this crime against humanity are known to be safely in the hands of those now taking charge.

"Mrs. Stuart, it now seems obvious why you were taken into protective custody following your harrowing ordeal in Israel. Can you share with the world what it was like, and what you want to happen now?"

"I will give a complete report of our kidnapping and the conditions under which we were held, but only to be released after this tragic situation is resolved. Let me just say that the experience was a terrible nightmare from hell.

"I also want to state that my husband is not responsible for what has happened. He has been under a hypnotic spell, one which has been administered by agents for the OWSC. I have been informed that as we speak, Julian is being rescued, and will be returning to me soon. Those responsible for this macabre conspiracy wished to use the depravity of economics, a condition which they themselves manufactured, to enslave us. We have not been enlightened, but blinded. They have taken evil and masqueraded it as good. They have taken the need for a New Age of peace and harmony and used it to bring bondage."

Thirty minutes prior to the broadcast, in Rome, five members of the Metsada Special Forces were utilizing codes provided by Angelica to enter the palace of the king without a hitch. Darts were blown through tubes to immobilize the guards. Both Julian and Monique had been captured and carried to a waiting Sikorsky X2 helicopter owned by the OWSC. The pilot, highly trained by the Italian army, had been commandeered and forced to fly them to a private air strip near Turin, where they were now on a Lear headed for Heathrow. The entire operation, a vital part of the overall mission dubbed "Save the King" took a grand total of 25 minutes.

In the posh bunker in Jerusalem, Joshua Bilderberger paced the floor. Suddenly his cell rang.

"Did you see the television report?" Jordon screamed.

"That's not even the worst of our worries. I was just about to call you. You must be out of touch with Julian. I've just received a call from the Palace Guard. They've taken Julian and his queen! How could we be so overtaken? They even know about this bunker. How could the "powers that be" not be in charge of our own destiny?"

"What will you do?"

"For now, I'm staying here—out of sight! There are always the secret chambers which are not on our blueprints."

"But whoever is behind this is now holding the cards. They have Angelica, the manuscript, and now my son, the king!"

"I suggest that you find a port of protection. You needn't be taken as well."

"I've got to go. Someone is at the door."

# Chapter Seventy

---

Jordon peered through the peep hole at his plush London penthouse. Armed guards were displaying badges; what type badges, he didn't know and couldn't care less. Dashing to his private voice-activated elevator, he quickly entered, giving the command to go down to the fifth floor where his private helicopter sat waiting on a pad extending from the side of the building.

On board the Lear, a phyciatrist was examining Julian, who, along with Monique, had been stunned by a taser and smothered with a nose-full of ether.

"Here it is," he puffed. Feeling about his forehead the doctor had discovered a tiny, unnatural lump. "The king has had a microchip implanted which was evidently programmed to both control him and track his movements. It likely also contains a world of information which we need to help us convict the perpetrators. This kind of devise was originally designed as a wartime aid to track prisoners, before evolving into a total control mechanism."

The commander of the operation nodded his head. "No surprise to me."

Knowing that he had to regroup, Mahmud Hemmati was en route to Afghanistan. He was no match for Bilderberger's wrath, much less the surreal forces that had captured control of the news media.

As Jordan Stuart emerged onto the pad, his mouth flew open. The opposing forces were waiting.

In his getaway resort in Crete, General Lorraine met a similar fate, as had both Dr. Baldwin and Mike Montgomery in London.

On the worldwide news, the magnetic report continued.

"Another intriguing development in this case has just been handed to me by a trusted correspondent," said the anchor, "Since the takeover by the One World Government, an organization called 'Citizens for Truth and Justice' has been conducting a secret investigation into the forces behind this unparalleled regime, and how someone could come out of nowhere, so to speak, and convince the world that a new savior was on the scene. The claims of this powerful group, called by conspiracy terrorists the 'Illuminati,' or in some cases, 'the powers that be,' claimed that Julian Stuart not only had right to rule based on the Gnostic prophecy, which we now know was a fraud—an ancient document altered during the Middle Ages—but also based on the claim that he was a descendant of a holy bloodline descending from either Jesus and Mary Magdalene, or as some claim, from Jesus' brother James.

"At any rate, he was claimed to have been the heir to the throne of David. This fantastic claim has now been shown to be a fabrication. Firstly, there is evidence to show that the Gnostic documents were likely manufactured by fanatics looking for publicity. Secondly, and even more compelling, are the DNA proofs. As many of you know, especially those who have been involved in various DNA family projects over the past several years, widely publicized on the Internet, the male Y chromosome is passed from father-to-son throughout history, indicating male ancestry.

"A project by the Cohen family showed that they were descended from Moses brother,

Aaron, the father of the keepers of the Jewish temple, from the tribe of Levi, the priestly tribe as indicated in the Torah. These are of the haplogroup J, and are exclusively either subgroups J2 or J1.

"A significant amount of Jewish men are of the G haplogroup: still others are H. A few have even been Q. While both Ashkenazi and Sephardic Jews have sometimes been R1, there has been much dispute as to the origin of some of these groups. It was widely reported that the Ashkenazim were a European tribe of pagan origin, a group who merely converted to the Jewish faith.

"The right to the throne was said to come through the Merovingian Frankish rulers of the seventh century. They also claimed this 'divine right' to rule as descendants of this proclaimed 'holy' royal line.

"A DNA test was conducted on bones of Frankish Merovingian warriors unearthed in Ergolding, Bavaria in 2009. In those tests, three were R1b, and two were G2. Much speculation about this DNA caused division among amateur researchers and experts alike because no one could prove that the actual Merovingian kings were either haplogroup.

"Now, a shocking new discovery makes the answer to this crystal clear. We received a call yesterday from a DNA testing facility in Rosdorf, Germany. Bones recently unearthed in Soissons, France, the first Merovingian capitol, were positively identified as those of the Merovingians, not only by their armor, but also by distinctive markings on their sarcophagi. These have been proven to be of the rare G2a haplogroup, not R1b, which is the most common Western European group.

"Who knows for certain whom these powerful rulers really were? The One World Scientific Committee made no secret of the fact that the haplotype of the Stuart dynasty, and the king, himself, is R1b1. We have since learned that both his supposed death and resurrection were a farce.

"Ladies and gentlemen, the Citizens for Truth and Justice, with the aid of various core groups from all major world powers, have just declared the current government to be null and void, In turn, they are calling on all individual heads of state to join them in taking our world back.

"I'm now being told that we have the head of that organization to address us. We

take you live to Jerusalem and Akim Manassas!"

# Chapter Seventy-one

"Ladies and gentlemen, beloved citizens of our awesome planet, a short time ago, a number of daring missions were carried out simultaneously. While it is not perfect, our world has again been made a better place in which to live.

"Each major leader of the conspiracy for One World Government and domination has been taken into captivity. Just as those dictators in history who thought that they were indestructible, these individuals, as well, are not. The existence of our vast group has been kept hidden for scores of years, just as had that of our opposition.

This investigation did not begin when the world government came into power — it has been ongoing for quite a long time. Our members, even more so than those of the One World Powers, come from all walks of life. They are doctors, lawyers, milkmen and teachers. They are workers in homeless shelters; they are black, white, brown, yellow and red. They are Kiwanians, Rotarians, Freemasons and Ruritan Club members. They are Christians, Jews, Muslims, Buddhists, Hindus, among other faiths, and some who claim no faith at all. Yes, they are diversified, but they are all persons dedicated to keeping the world free of tyranny such as recently slipped up on us. Our investigation into the claims of the One World Government could not have been completed without the help of some extraordinary people, some of whom have only recently been made a part of our force for Truth.

"Could it be that these men who carried out this scheme really believed that they were doing the right thing for our world? Could they have been duped by an ancient conspiracy that has been overly carried down through the centuries? Indeed, I see these as having been distinct possibilities.

"I would like to offer special thanks to a young American District Attorney named Daniel St. James, who will later testify in the impending hearings and trials of the individuals responsible for this façade.

It is also imperative that I thank Mario Angelica, former Chief of Security for the OWSC, and Special Envoy to the Vatican, for his daring efforts above and beyond the call of duty.

"In addition, there is my special long-time friend, and a member of our group, Dr. David Ben-Dura. It was due to his unsurpassed expertise that we were able to prove the forgery of the mysterious manuscript.

"And last, but certainly not least, there is General Yosef ben Canaan of Israel. It was he who was successful in capturing the head of the conspiracy, Dr. Joshua Bilderberger, himself, who is now in captivity in Tel Aviv. The General had been serving undercover in a secret bunker as head of security for the past two months. It was he who also aided the true wife of 'King' Julian Stuart, who was controlled by his father under the direction of Dr. Bilderberger. General ben Canaan was in charge of the entire operation, 'Save the King.' Julian Stuart is now being deprogrammed by doctors of our organization. All world leaders, many of whom were not happy with their new roles, will be meeting in an upcoming summit at a yet undisclosed location to be briefed and returned to their previous non-controlled positions.

No, the utopian age has not arrived, nor has the true 'messiah' come. However, in an imperfect world we can once again have hope.

Many noble goals were given mention by the deceptive regime. Good ideas in the hands of evil people produce twisted results. A good deal of these goals will undoubtedly be considered by the world leaders as they face the uncertain future of our world

In no way do we wish to have control over the separate governments of our world, but we will be glad to aid any leader wishing for such support. Our organization has been and continues to be funded by donations from our members.

I now return you to your previously scheduled programming."

In the new government building in the old city of Jerusalem, the Israeli Prime Minister's countenance was ghostly pale as he spoke. "What do we do now?"

"We now await the true messiah," Rabbi Ginsberg said in a bland tone. "Some- day he shall appear. Let's pray that we are never so easily deceived again."

In Richmond, Daniel was taking Klarissa for a joyous reunion with her husband. As her heart was singing; his mind was bending in thankful prayer.

"A lie gets halfway around the world before the truth has a chance to put its pants on."

-Winston Churchill

"The scientific concept of dictatorship means nothing else but this: power without limit, resting directly upon force, reinstated by no laws, absolutely unrestricted by rules."

-Vladimir I. Lenin, *A Contribution to the History of the Question of Dictatorship*

"[The goal is] nothing less than to create a world system of financial control in private hands able to dominate the political system of each country and the economy of the world as a whole."

-Carroll Quigley, *Tragedy and Hope,* 1966

"In short, 'the house of world order' will have to be built from the bottom up rather than from the top down."

-Richard N. Gardner, *The Road to World Order, Foreign Affairs,* April, 1974